I0556404

Twisted Starr 3
The Final Chapter

Twisted Starr 3
The Final Chapter

BY

TRACY WILSON

http://beautifulpublications.com

Published by
Beautiful Publications LLC
Stratford, CT 06614

PRINT ISBN: 978-1-7331792-3-2
EBOOK ISBN: 978-1-7334002-3-7

Printed in the United States of America

Dedication

I dedicate this series to Starr.

Chapter 1

"Hey Keisha..."

"Girl – what's wrong?"

"Nothing..."

"Oh so you just knocked on my door for nothing?"

"If you're not up for company I'll just come back another time..."

"Git yo' ass in here..." Keisha said as she grabbed Beautiee into a hug... and Beautiee started crying...

"Is Troy here?"

"No..."

"Good..." Beautiee said as she went into the kitchen and started making coffee. Keisha watched her intently without speaking. Beautiee made coffee, got the cups, creamer, sugar, and put everything on the table, and then sat down...

"Bazil..." Keisha said as they made their coffee and started drinking...

"I wish I wasn't pregnant..."

"Oh damn – what the fuck happened?"

"Oh no – I'm just saying I wish I wasn't pregnant because I want a drink..." Beautiee laughed...

1

"Oh thank God – ya'll be scaring the shit outta me!" Keisha laughed...

"I'm sorry..."

"You ain't gotta be sorry – life happens..."

"Damn sure does..."

"So... you wanna tell me what you were crying about?"

"How much coffee you have left?"

"I have espresso if you need something stronger..."

"Oh hell yea!"

"Okay – we'll finish this and then I'll make some espresso..."

"Okay..."

"Beautiee..." Keisha said as she took her hand... "This isn't good for you... or the baby..."

"I know..."

"What's going on?"

"A lot..." Keisha got up from the table and put on the espresso maker and started the pot...

"I can listen while I'm making coffee..."

"Starr has a job..."

"That's good..."

"She works at the University in New Haven..."

"Okay..."

"She works Monday through Thursday - 8:30 – 4:30 - Friday 8:30 to 1:30 – Saturday 9 to 1..."

"She likes the job?"

"She loves it..."

"That's good..."

2

"She's really sweet…"

"That's nice…"

"I wish she was my daughter…"

"Aww…"

"They came to see us on Tuesday…"

"Starr and Chandler…"

"They good?"

"They went to City Hall…"

"They got their marriage license?"

"Yea…"

"They set a date?"

"Yea…"

"When they getting' married?"

"June 6th…"

"Damn – when did you plan on sending invitations?"

"I'm not…"

"So we're not invited?"

"You stupid…" Beautiee laughed…

"Okay – I'ma put this on my calendar…"

"It's in Boston at the Taylor Bed & Breakfast – they plan everything – you just show up…"

"Oh that's nice – they book it yet?"

"I took care of their wedding and their honeymoon on Tuesday…"

"Damn – I wish I knew you when we got married…" Keisha laughed…

"I love Starr – she's so in love – she's so happy – I just wanted to do that for her…"

"You did that for Bazil too…"

"Yea…"

"Here..." Keisha said as she put the espresso on the table...

"Keisha — you want me to drink this straight up?"

"Drink!"

"Okay, okay!" Beautiee laughed as she drank it... "Uggh!"

"You gonna talk now or do I have to make you drink another shot?"

"Fuck it — hit me again — but this time you're drinking with me..."

"Aiight — bet!" Keisha said as they both took a shot of espresso...

"Uugh!" they both said in unison...

"Starr got an eviction notice..."

"Oh shit!"

"Her mother was supposed to be out by Friday or Starr was gonna get evicted and lose her Section 8..."

"Her mother had to go to the shelter?"

"She was..."

"What happened?"

"The realtor called — Starr got her keys to her new place on Thursday..."

"Starr got an apartment?"

"Bazil bought her a co-op in Downtown Bridgeport..."

"Oh wow — he know her mother's staying there?"

"Yea..."

"And he's okay with that?"

"He wasn't... but I talked to him..."

"Chandler told them both he was tired of Starr being in the middle of their shit!"

"No he didn't!"

"Yes girl – here's the funny part though..." I laughed...

"Tell me – I wanna laugh too..."

"Chandler told them if they kept putting Starr in the middle of their shit he would make sure they didn't see Starr again!"

"Aaaahaaaa! Aaaahaaaa!" they both laughed...

"Wait – Chandler thinks he can stop Bazil – hell – nobody stops Bazil!" she laughed...

"Girl – I ain't done..."

"Oh hell – my stomach..."

"Bazil told him he couldn't stop him from seeing his daughter..." Beautiee laughed... "and Chandler said try me!"

"Aaaahaaaa! Aaaahaaaa!" they both laughed...

"You lyin!"

"No girl!"

"Go 'head Chandler!"

"I know – right?"

"This is good – but you still ain't tell me what Bazil did..."

"I'm getting' to it!"

"Okay – go 'head..."

"So... Chandler pulled out a lease..."

"No!"

"Yes girl – and he told Mary Bazil made you an offer – and you're gonna take it!"

7

"I fuckin' love Chandler!"

"Me too girl!"

"What'd she say?"

"She tried it – but Chandler told her Starr doesn't need her Section 8 anymore – the rent is only paid until the end of May – so she doesn't have a choice – unless she wants to go to the shelter – but don't expect Starr to come visit!"

"Oh shit!" Keisha said as they high-fived... "Bazil put him up to that?"

"No girl – it was all Chandler..."

"I love it, I love it, I love it! Did she sign it?"

"She signed it..."

"Yeesss!"

"So everybody's happy – Bazil comes home..." Beautiee said as she started crying...

"What happened?"

"He called me to the kitchen... he has fruit, meat, cheese, sparkling cider, balloons, roses..."

"Aww..."

"He tells me he did that for me because of everything I did for his daughter... he tells me how much he loves me... I was so happy..."

"Okay – I'm confused – if you were so happy..."

"I'm getting to that..."

"Oh my God – I can't take it..."

"So... that was Tuesday and Wednesday... now we get to Thursday..."

"Okay..."

"Sheddi calls..."

"Okay – wait – who's Sheddi?"

"The real estate agent..."

"Okay..."

"So she says they can close Friday morning..."

"Okay..."

"So we're celebrating..."

"Yall fuckin'..." Keisha laughed...

"Yea..." Beautiee said as she took out her phone and showed Keisha the picture of Bazil kissing her stomach in the shower...

"Oh wow... that's dope..."

"That was Friday morning..." Beautiee said as she started tearing up. Keisha took Beautiee's hand and Beautiee kept talking... "So they went to the closing... they got the keys... and Bazil came home... I heard him come in... I called him... he didn't answer me... so I went in the kitchen... I threw my arms around his neck... I kissed him... and..." Keisha started rubbing Beautiees arm as she cried... "He pushed me away from him... and... told... me... to... leave... him... alone..." Keisha got up from the table, went to the bathroom, got a box of tissues... and came back into the kitchen...

"Damn – I know that hurt your feelings – that shit hurt my feelings..." she said as she wiped her eyes along with Beautiee...

"I went in the library and I turned on the computer to do some writing... and Starr called me..."

"What'd she say?"

"She asked me what was wrong – and I told her nothing..."

"She knew you was lyin'..."

"She asked me why I was acting so funny – first her father, then her mother, now me..."

"Something happened at that closing..."

"Starr said her father started acting funny after he had an argument with Smalls..."

"Oh shit..."

"So I went in the kitchen to talk to Bazil... he wasn't there but he left his jacket in the kitchen... and I picked it up... and this letter fell out..." Beautiee said as she started crying again..." That Triflin' Bitch is suing Bazil for back child support..." Beautiee cried...

"So... Smalls served Bazil... at the closing?"

"Yea..." Beautiee sniffed...

"And Bazil comes home... and pushes you away..."

"Yea..."

"See – that's that bullshit!"

"Exactly..."

"He needs to apologize..."

"He apologized yesterday... but I pushed him away from me..."

"You did? Why?"

"I pushed him away because I'm tired..."

"You're tired? Oh shit..."

"I told him you're sorry – and I'm tired..."

"Did he try to explain?"

"I told him I didn't want to hear it..."

10

"Oh damn – that's not like you..."

"I'm tired Keisha – I asked him how many fuckin' times do we have to go through shit before he fuckin' gets it?"

"You right..."

"He pushed me away... after everything we've been through... after everything I've done... and that hurt..."

"Damn Beautiee... I'm sorry..."

"It took everything in me not to choke that Triflin' Bitch yesterday..."

"Wait – what?"

"I promised Starr we would go shopping for wedding dresses... and I promised her I'd pick up her mother..."

"Oh hell no – you good..."

"What was I supposed to do Keisha?"

"And Bazil pushed you away from him... and you cryin' – that mutha fucka should be cryin'..."

"He was..."

"Good..."

"I love him so much... but I'm tired... he hurts me – he's sorry – then he hurts me again... and I'm tired..."

"You're pregnant too..."

"I know..."

"You're emotional..."

"I've always been emotional..."

"So whatchu gonna do?"

"I slept in the guest room last night... and I locked the door so Bazil couldn't get in..."

"Oh shit! You that mad?"

"Keisha?"

"Yea?"

"I had to lock the door…"

"Why?"

"It was the only way I could stop myself from jumpin' on his dick…"

"Oh so you not mad…"

"It really hurt my feelings… and I'm really tired…"

"You not gonna talk about it?"

"I just wanna see Starr and Chandler get married… she was so happy yesterday trying on dresses…"

"I bet her mother was too…"

"Yea…"

"She didn't say anything to you?"

"She tried – and I shut her down…"

"You did?"

"I told her don't open her fuckin' mouth about my husband – and don't tell me how sorry you are – show me – fix it!"

"Girl – I'on know if I could do it – you good…"

"If it wasn't for Starr…"

"You really love her…"

"I do… she's actually worried about me… she told me she knew something was going on with me and her father and it made her sad…"

"Aww…"

"I can't ruin her wedding Keisha…"

"So you not gonna tell her?"

"No..."

"What about Bazil? Ya'll need to talk..."

"Girl... I don't need to talk..." I laughed...

"Oh Lord – I can't - y'all make me sick..." she laughed... "but for real though – he didn't mean to hurt your feelings..."

"Keisha?"

"What?"

"Did you just defend Bazil?"

"I know – right?" she laughed...

"I'll talk to him..."

"Good..."

Beautiee went back in the house, she went straight upstairs to the guest room... and bust out laughing. While she was at Keisha & Troy's house, Bazil took the door off the guest room to keep her from locking him out and, to be honest, it made her smile. She shook her head, sat down on the bed, and saw an envelope addressed to her, so she picked it up, took out his letter and started reading...

Dear Beautiee,

I'm sorry. I know you're tired – tired of me hurting you - tired of me being sorry for hurting you – and tired of me hurting you – please believe me – I swear I don't mean to – I just can't help it. I know that's no excuse – but I'm being honest – and I'm trying. All you wanted to do was love me and I should've let you – but I was in so much pain I couldn't let you love me. When I pushed you away from me I was being selfish – but I can't help that either – I was too deep in my feelings at the moment to realize how hurt you were – I know that's no excuse – but I need you to understand it had nothing to do with you and everything to do with me. I've never had a woman come and comfort me – especially after I pushed them away – the way you did. It's easy when I'm loving you and comforting you because I'm the man – I'm supposed to do that – but it's hard for me to be vulnerable – especially in difficult moments. When I pushed you away it wasn't because I didn't want you – I'll always want you – it was because I was angry that Mary got to me – again – I was angry at myself for letting her get to me – and I was angry at myself for being weak – and instead of telling you how I was feeling I pushed you away. Starr was so happy at the closing and I had to sit there and pretend that I was happy when the truth is – I wanted to choke the shit out of Conrad for taking the case – and I also wanted to choke the shit outta my friend – my brother – Smalls – for serving me that fuckin' paper.

Now that you know how I feel – please forgive me. I can't promise you I won't hurt you again – but I can promise you I'm gonna let you love me – because I need you to.

Love,

Bazil

Beautiee sat there and cried. She was so happy Bazil shared what he was going through and what he was feeling, she took out the same pad and pen he used to write her that letter and she wrote one back...

Dear Bazil,

Thank you. I'm crying as I'm writing this – not because I'm hurt – but because I'm happy. I'm happy that you let me know what you were going through and how you were feeling – and I'm sorry you were hurting. I know it's hard for you to be vulnerable but as you said – you're a man – and just like the rest of us – you have a heart – and feelings – and you can be hurt too. I'm also sorry you've never known comfort from another woman – but I'm happy to know that I'm able to comfort you when you need it most – and I will comfort you whenever you need me to. When I read that letter I was hurt for all of us – and I was hurt for your friend – your brother – Smalls – because I know it broke his heart to have to serve you that paper. You said in your letter you wanted to choke the shit outta Conrad – well – I wanna choke the shit outta Mary. It was all I could do to keep my composure yesterday when we picked Mary up to go shopping for wedding dresses – and I had to check her too – she brought your name up and I told her don't open your fuckin' mouth about my husband – and don't tell me how sorry you are – show me – fix it!

I swear if Starr wasn't getting married – but she is – and I love her – and I love you – but when this wedding is over – we're going into battle – and we're going to take that Triflin Bitch down together.

Love,

Beautiee

Beautiee took her letter, put it in an envelope, went into the bedroom, handed it to Bazil, and sat down on the bed beside him as he read it. He started crying and she cried too. He took her face in his hands and kissed her and when he did, they couldn't keep their hands off each other...

"Bazil..."
"Beautiee...
"Bazil..."
"Beautiee...
"Hmmm...."
"Ugghhh...
"Hmmm..."
"Ugghh..."
"Yeess..."
"Fuck... shit... shit..."

"Oh God..." Beautiee and Bazil held on to each other for dear life and fucked for the next hour...

"Ooohhh...."

"Ummppphhh..."

"Ooohhh...

"Mmmppphhh..." It was a battle between the sexes as Bazil and Beautiee took turns flipping each other around on the bed and when Bazil put Beautiee's legs up on his shoulders and started fuckin' her hard and deep... she lost it...

"Oh God... Bazil! I'm cumming!"

"Uugghhh! Uuugghhh! Uugghh!" Bazil held Beautiee in position for a few moments before he put her legs down and lay down beside her...

"Bazil..." she breathed...

"Yes... Beautiee..." he breathed as he kissed her...

"That... was... so... fuckin... good..."

"I know..." he said as he smiled mischievously...

"Fuck you..." she laughed...

"You just did..."

"I love you..."

"I love you too..."

"You ready for battle?"

"With you by my side? Hell yea!" Bazil said as he pulled Beautiee into a kiss and they continued kissing and holding each other.

Chapter 2

"I can't wait to get this over with..." Mary said as she rode the bus to Trumbull... "Oh good – I'm here..." she said as she got off the bus and walked to Conrad's office. When she got there she opened the door and walked inside.

"Mary – please come into my office..." Conrad said as he smiled at Mary and led her into his office...

"Where's Dominique?"

"I gave her the day off... it's just you... and me..."

"Mr. Cox... I..."

"Ssshhh... I won't hurt you... I promise..."

"Mr. Cox... I'm flattered... but..."

"I need you to do something for me..." Conrad said as he went up close to Mary and held up a pen...

"What's this for?"

"I need you to sign this paper saying that you're withdrawing the lawsuit..."

"That's it?"

"Sign – right here..." Conrad said as he pointed where he needed her to sign..."

"Thank you..." Conrad said as he walked up behind Mary and started kissing her on the back of her neck...

"Mr. Cox... please..."

"I need you..." he said as he kissed her neck... "to go in the bathroom... take off your clothes... and walk back out here naked..."

"Please Mr. Cox... please don't make me do this... I'll go through with the lawsuit..."

"It's too late for that..."

"Please... I'll do anything you want... just don't hurt me..."

"That's more like it..." Conrad said as he held her and kissed her... "Now... I don't want to ask you again... please... go take off your clothes... and come back..."

"Okay... okay..." Mary whispered as she went into the bathroom, took off her clothes, and came back out naked...

"Take your arms down... come stand in front of me..."

"Okay..." Mary whispered as she started crying. Conrad stood up, went towards her, and pulled her into a kiss. Mary started shaking...

"Stop crying... I'm not going to hurt you... I promise..."

"You promise?"

"Yes..."

"So you're not going to rape me?"

"No..."

"Okay..."

"Now... do you think you're pretty?"

"I don't understand..."

"Do you think you're pretty?"

"Yes..."

"Good... because you are... now... come over here..."

"Okay..." Conrad turned her towards the full length mirror behind his door, stood behind her, and held her against him so she could see him behind her in the mirror...

"Now..." Conrad said as he held her and whispered in her ear... "I told you... I only take cases I can win... unless you have a retainer to pay me..."

"I'm sorry..."

"I don't want an apology..." he said as he rubbed her stomach... "I want $50,000... plus my legal fees..."

"Can't I just pay you for serving the papers?"

"It's too late for that..." Conrad said as he moved his hands up to her breasts and cupped them...

"Please... please don't do this..."

"Please don't do what?" Conrad asked as he moved his hands down to her waist...

"Please don't hurt me..."

"I promised you I wouldn't..."

"Okay..."

"But you withdrew your lawsuit... $150,000... one third of that belongs to me... plus legal fees..."

"I don't have any money..."

"That's not my problem..." Conrad said as he moved his hands down to her ass..."

"I'll work for you... for free... to pay you..."

"That'll take too long..." Conrad said as he moved his hands to her pelvis..."

"Please... just tell me what I can do... I'll do anything..." Mary said as she started crying...

"That's what I wanted to hear..." Conrad said as he turned her around to face him... "Now... go get dressed..." he said as he let her go and he sat back at his desk...

"Okay..." Mary whispered as she went into the bathroom, got dressed, and came back into the office with Conrad...

"Now... you owe me $50,000... plus legal feels..."

"Okay..."

"If you run me my money in 10 days... I'll waive the legal fees – if not..."

"What?"

"You'll work with an associate of mine... until your debt is paid..."

"Oh hell no..."

"Oh hell yes..."

"Fuck it – you can have the pussy if you want it – I'd rather do that..." she said as she started to take off her clothes...

"You don't understand..." Conrad said...

21

"I'm not selling my ass..."

"I won't force you... but if you don't run me my money in 10 days..." Conrad said as he stood up from behind the desk and approached her... "and if you're not willing to sell your ass..." he said as he pulled her close and held her tight against him... "then I'll take out an insurance policy... you'll meet with an untimely death... and I'll collect..." he said as he kissed her... "You see... I'ma get my money... one way or the other..."

"Let go of me!" Mary snapped...

"Of course..." Conrad said as he let go of her and went and sat back behind his desk...

"Remember... 10 days..." he said as Mary ran out...

"Oh my God... what am I going to do? Please God... help me..."

"Figures... now that your greed and hatred have put you in a hole you can't climb out of... now you want my help..." God said...

"I know I've been greedy... what I did was spiteful... but I tried to fix it..."

"You tried to fix it after everything I did for you... you got out of prison... you have your daughter... you didn't have to go to a shelter... I made all this happen... for you... and yet... you still want more... you refuse to listen... you refuse to learn..."

"Please God – I swear – I won't do anything else – I've learned my lesson..."

"Sigh... Okay Mary... when you get home... call Jermoll..."

"I know what I'll do — I'll call Jermoll..." Mary said as she got on the bus and sat down. Mary stared out the window until it was time to get off the bus. "Thank God I'm home..." she said as she got off the bus, ran home, opened the door, and called Jermoll... "Jermoll?"

"Mary... what's wrong?"

"I... I..." she cried...

"Where are you?"

"I'm... home..." she cried...

"Text me the address — I'm on my way..." Jermoll said as he hung up... "Sarge?"

"Yes Thompson?"

"I need to go out for a bit — I'll be back..."

"Okay Thompson..." Chandler said as Jermoll made a beeline to Mary. When he got there Mary opened the door and threw her arms around him...

"Mary... what happened?"

"I'm in trouble..."

"What happened?"

"I have 10 days to come up with $50,000... or he'll kill me!" she cried...

"Who?"

"Conrad Cox..."

"The attorney?"

"Yes..."

"What... never mind... how?"

"I filed a lawsuit against Bazil... $150,000... for back child support..."

"Okay..."

"I withdrew the lawsuit..."

"Oh shit..."

"Now he wants $50,000... in 10 days... or I need to start selling my ass... and if I refuse... he'll kill me..."

"You won't have to do that Mary..."

"If I don't do it – he'll kill me!" Mary cried...

"Mary..." Jermoll whispered as he kissed her... "Listen to me..."

"Okay..."

"I'll give you the money..."

"What?"

"I'll give you the money..."

"You will?"

"Yes Mary..."

"I don't understand... why?"

"I've done a lot of things..."

"Jermoll..."

"I need to do something right... something for you..."

"Jermoll..." Mary breathed... "I had no idea..."

"Well now you do..." Jermoll breathed as he pulled Mary into a kiss, took her by the hand, and led her into the bedroom.

Chapter 3

"Beautiee..." Bazil whispered in her ear as he nibbled on her earlobe...

"Bazil... I'm tired..."

"Mmmmm....." Bazil moaned as he kissed her...

"Please... I'm tired..."

"Beautiee?"

"Yes Bazil?"

"Come here..." he said as he put his arm around her and she snuggled up underneath him...

"I'm sorry..."

"This isn't like you..."

"I know..."

"I'm worried..."

"Please... don't..."

"I can't help it..."

"I need you..." she whispered as she started crying...

"Please don't cry..." Bazil whispered as he started crying...

"You're not helping..."

"I'm sorry..."

"I'm sorry... I don't know what's wrong with me..." she cried...

"Please... stop... crying..." Bazil cried as he kissed her...

"I can't..."

"I'm calling Keisha..." Bazil said as he dialed Troy's number...

"You ready for today Bazil?" Troy asked as he answered his phone...

"Is Keisha there?"

"Bazil – what's wrong?"

"I don't know..."

"We're on our way..." Troy said as he hung up...

"Keisha's coming?" Beautiee asked...

"They both are..."

"Okay..." Beautiee sniffed as she sat up...

"What's wrong?" Keisha asked...

"Bazil needs us..."

"What the fuck he do now?" Keisha sighed as she got up outta bed and went to the bathroom...

"I don't know..." Troy answered as he went into the bathroom, peed, and went over to the sink...

"He better have some coffee – gettin' me up out my bed for some bullshit – I swear – he lucky you love him..."

"You love him too..." Troy laughed...

"Shut up Troy..." Keisha laughed as she went over to Troy, put her arms around him, and kissed him...

"You keep kissing me like that..." he said as he kissed her... "I'll do whatever you want..."

"Damn – why the fuck we gotta go over there right now – you makin' me wet n shit..."

"Oh yea?" Troy asked as he pulled Keisha into another kiss and palmed her ass...

"Troy..." Keisha breathed... "We gotta go..."

"Just let me put the head in..." Troy breathed as he pushed Keisha backwards towards the sink...

"Troy..." Keisha moaned as Troy picked her up, put her on the edge of the sink, and opened her legs...

"Keisha..." Troy moaned as he eased himself inside her and started thrusting...

"Troy... shit..." Keisha moaned as she held him tighter and rode his dick...

"Uggh... Uggh... Uggh..."

"Huh... Huh... Huh..."

"Damn this shit feel good..."

"Oh shit... you gon' make me cum..."

"Cum for me..."

"Huh... Huh... Huh... Troy... Troy..."

"Fuck... I'm cumming with you..."

"Troy... Troy... Troy... Aaaaaggghhhh!"

"Uggh! Uggh! Uggh! Uggh! Uggh! Uuuggghhhh!"

"Troy..." Keisha whispered as tears came down her face...

"Keisha..." Troy whispered as tears came down his face... "I love you so much..."

"I love you too..." she breathed as she wrapped her legs around Troy and they held each other...

"I don't wanna go..." he breathed as he started kissing her...

"Troy..."

"Keisha..."

"Troy... stop..."

"Okay..."

"Help me down off the sink..."

"Okay..." Troy said as he lifted Keisha down off the sink and she put her legs down...

"I wonder if they ever did it on the sink?"

"Ask her..." Troy said as he turned on the water and started shaving..."

"I'ma see what's going on first..." Keisha said as she turned on the water and started brushing her teeth...

"Let's make this quick..."

"Why we gotta make it quick?"

"I wanna get it in again before we go to the wedding..."

"Bazil?"

"Yes Beautiee?"

"Will you bring me some coffee?"

"You're not coming downstairs?"

"No..." Bazil went upstairs to get Beautiee...

"Where's my coffee?"

"It's downstairs..." he said as he extended his hand to help Beautiee stand up...

28

"I don't wanna go downstairs – I wanna stay in bed..." she sighed...

"I wish you could..." he said as he kissed her... "But today is their wedding day..."

"Oh shoot – I need to call Starr and..."

"You... need... to... let... me... take... care... of... you..." he breathed between kisses...

"Yes My Thirst Quencher..." Beautiee sighed as she smiled...

"There... you... are..." he said as he wrapped his arm around her and led her out the bedroom...

"Bazil! Open the door!" Troy yelled as he banged on the door...

"I'm coming!" he yelled as he came downstairs with Beautiee. Beautiee went in the kitchen and sat down as Bazil answered the door...

"Good morning..." Bazil said as he let them in...

"Good morning – you good?"

"Not really..."

"Good morning Bazil..." Keisha said...

"Good morning Keisha..." Bazil said as he walked into the kitchen and they followed...

"Thank God you made coffee – Beautiee – what's wrong?"

"I don't know..." Beautiee whispered as she started crying...

"You want some coffee?"

"Yea..." Beautiee sniffed...

"Okay – y'all want coffee too?"

"Yes – thank you..." Bazil said. Keisha made four cups of coffee and set them on the table...

"Y'all go in the living room so we can talk..." Keisha said...

"C'mon Troy..." Bazil said as he got up and Troy followed...

"Keisha..." Beautiee whispered...

"Yea?"

"Something's wrong with me..."

"I know..."

"Keisha... you don't understand..."

"What's wrong Beautiee?"

"This morning... Bazil wanted some..."

"And?"

"Keisha..."

"What girl – what?"

"I told him I was tired..."

"Wai-a-min... you didn't want no dick?"

"Noo..." she whispered as she started crying...

"Beautiee – you alright..." Keisha said as she rubbed her hand...

"No I'm not – I'm irritable – I'm tired – all I wanna do is go to bed – and stay there!"

"Girl – you getting' ready to have that baby..."

"You think so?"

"I know so..."

"I hope so..."

"See – I told you – you alright..."

"Mary told me Starr was pre-mature..."

"She did?"

"Yea..."

"You asked her?"

"Yea..."

"Yea – you gon' have that baby any day – how many months are you?"

"I'm eight months today..."

"Aww shit – we gon' have to watch you..."

"I have so much to do – I gotta make sure Starr..."

"Beautiee – I know you love her – but she has a mother – ain't she gonna be at the wedding?"

"Yea..."

"Let her mother do something then!"

"I just want Starr to have the perfect wedding..."

"She's marrying Chandler – it doesn't get more perfect than that..."

"You're right..." Beautiee said as she smiled...

"That's better – now give me your phone..."

"Here..." Beautiee said as she handed Keisha her phone...

"Hey Beautiee..." Chandler answered...

"It's Keisha..."

"Beautiee alright?"

"She's fine – you need to pick up Mary – and make sure y'all get there early – Beautiee wants Starr's wedding to be perfect..."

"What about Charles and Theresa?"

31

"Them too..."

"Okay – I'm on it – see you later..."

"Thank you Keisha..." Beautiee said...

"You're welcome – now – it's still early – you're gonna go upstairs and lay down for another hour – got it?"

"Yes Maam..."

"Okay – we'll be back in an hour..." Keisha said as she got up and Beautiee went upstairs... "Troy?"

"Yea Keisha?"

"We're gonna go get ready – then we're gonna come back and make sure they're ready..."

"Okay..." Troy said as he got up, went to the door, and Bazil followed...

"Is she alright Keisha?" Bazil asked...

"No – but she will be..."

"What can I do?"

"I told her to go lay down for an hour – we'll be back – go lay down with her..." she said as she left with Troy. Bazil went upstairs, went into the bedroom, and smiled when he saw Beautiee sleeping...

"I love you..." he whispered as he lay down behind her and held her the same way he held her on their first night together.

Chapter 4

"Ladies – let's go!" Beautiee said...

"I'm coming!" Starr squealed as she came into the dressing room...

"Starr – I need you to take these bags to your room and come right back – we need to get your hair done and get you ready for your husband..."

"Okay!" she squealed as she grabbed the bags and ran downstairs to their room. When she came out, she ran right into Chandler...

"Hey..." Chandler said as he pulled her into a kiss...

"Hey..." Starr breathed...

"We're getting married..."

"I know..."

"Starr – let's go!" Beautiee yelled...

"I'm coming!" Starr yelled as she flew upstairs...

"Aiight guys – let's go!" Bazil said...

"Where we goin'?" Charles asked...

"In the dressing room guys..." Darryl's assistant said as he stuck his head out the room...

"You ready Chandler?" Bazil asked as they all went into the room...

"Hell yea!"

"Me too..." Bazil said as he pulled Chandler into a hug...

"Dad..." Chandler said as he started crying...

"Don't start that shit!" Charles laughed...

"Shut up!" Chandler laughed...

"I was a nervous wreck on my wedding day..." Troy said...

"We all were..." Smalls said...

"I cried right along with Beautiee..." Bazil said...

"Oh my God... look at my Baby..." Mary whispered as she started to cry...

"Mommy... please don't cry..." Starr said as she started crying...

"I love you so much..." Mary said as they hugged each other...

"I love you too Mommy..." Starr cried...

"Aiight – break it up – Mary – get dressed – Starr – get your garter belt on – matter fact – Mary – put this on her thigh..." Keisha said...

"Yes Maam..." Mary laughed...

"Theresa – you look pretty!" Starr exclaimed...

"Starr..." Theresa said as they started hugging each other...

"I love you..." Starr said...

"I love you too..."

"Is this where we get ready?" Josefina asked as she came inside...

"Yes – c'mon in..." Beautiee said...

"Oh ... una novia tan hermosa ..." Josefina said as she took Starr's hands...

"Thank you..." Starr said...

"You speak Spanish Starr?" Beautiee asked...

"No – but I've heard that before..."

"What'd she say?"

"She said I'm a beautiful bride..." Starr sighed...

"Si..." Josefina said as she got dressed...

"Beautiee – you alright?" Keisha asked...

"I'm better than I was – thanks Keisha...

"You're welcome – y'all ready?"

"Ready!" they all said in unison...

"Okay ladies – let's go!" Beautiee said as they all went downstairs...

"You look good Chandler..." Bazil said...

"Thanks Dad – you look good too..."

"Look at you!" Charles said...

"You lookin' sharp Charles!" Chandler said...

"Ahem!" Troy interrupted...

"Aww shit!" Charles said...

"Okay Smalls – I see you!" Troy said...

"We ready?" Bazil asked...

"We ready!" they all said in unison...

"Okay – let's go!" Bazil said as they all went downstairs...

Chapter 5

My father walked me down the aisle and I burst into tears as Chandler started singing 'You Are' by Charlie Wilson, to me...

"Butterflies is what I feel inside... And every time is like my first time... And I can't never find the words to say... You're the perfect girl... You were made for me..."

"Chandler..." I whispered as I cried and he continued singing...

"It's so easy to love you baby... We're compatible, incredible and natural we are... And girl I've never felt this way before... From the bottom of my heart... Baby girl I just wanna tell you that you are..."   My mother got up and caught me as I broke down in happy tears...

"The reason I love, the reason I trust... God sent me an angel... You are the best in the world... A wonderful girl... Knowing you by my side brings tears to my eyes... Starr..." Chandler sang as he started crying too... "Girl you had me from the moment I looked into your eyes... And I knew you were an angel but you were in disguise... Tell me how could I be so lucky... That you'd fall down from Heaven for me..."

"Chandler... I love... you... so... much..." I sobbed as my mother got me up to the front and I was standing in front of him and he continued singing...

"Some people search a lifetime and never find a true love..." my father, Charles, and Troy sang with Chandler...

"But Heaven cared enough for me to give me you... And now our hearts they beat together... Standing stronger here forever... You and I..."

"You and I... You and I... You and I..." My father, Charles, and Troy sang with Chandler...

"I just want you to know you are... The reason I love, the reason I trust... God sent me an angel... You are the best in the world... A wonderful girl... Knowing you by my side... And a man ain't supposed to cry..."

"But girl you are..." my father, Charles, and Troy sang with Chandler...

"The only woman I make love to..."

"Girl you are..." My father, Charles, and Troy sang with Chandler...

"The reason I come home at night..."

"Girl you are..." My father, Charles, and Troy sang with Chandler...

"You're all that I need in my life... And it almost feel... It's not fair... Loving you I don't care... You are..."

"You are..." My Father, Charles, and Troy sang with Chandler...

"You are... You are the reason I love, the reason I trust... God sent me an angel... You are the best in the world... A wonderful girl... You're a wonderful girl... Waoh Oh..."

"Baby you are..." My father, Charles, and Troy sang with Chandler...

"You're all that I am..."

"You are..." my father, Charles, and Troy sang...

"You're all that I need..."

"You are..." my father, Charles, and Troy sang...

"Baby heaven has sent you to me..."

"Baby you are..." my father, Charles and Troy sang...

"The one for me..."

"You are..." my father, Charles, and Troy sang...

"The air that I breathe..."

"You are..." my father, Charles, and Troy sang...

"Baby you are you are..."

"Ooohh Yeahh" my father, Charles, and Troy sang...

"You are, you are everyday to me baby... You're everything oh baby... Baby you are..." I looked out and everyone was crying. My father was crying pretty hard, and Chandler pulled him into a hug and cried with him as my mother pulled me into a hug along with Beautiee and they both cried with me. After everyone gathered themselves and wiped away their make-up along with their tears, the wedding continued. My father stood beside Chandler, my mother stood beside me, Beautiee stood beside my mother, and Darryl began the ceremony...

"Beloved... we are gathered here this afternoon to join Starr Osgood and Chandler Corbett in marriage. You have both come before me, expressed your desire to become husband and wife. Do you have rings?"

"Yes – we have rings..." Bazil said as he took two ring boxes out his pocket...

"Okay – take the rings out the boxes – Starr – you take his ring – Chandler – you take her ring..."

"Okay..." we both said in unison as I took his ring and he took mine...

"Who gives this woman to be married? Darryl asked...

"I do..." my father answered...

"Okay – Chandler – do you have anything you want to say to Starr?"

"Yes I do..." Chandler answered as he took my hands... "Starr...before I met you I was just a ladies man. That was fine when I was younger, but as I got older, I realized I no longer wanted to be a ladies man – I wanted to be a husband – so I prayed and asked God for a wife. When I saw you I was mesmerized by your beauty, your sweetness, and your innocence. When you chose to have coffee with me, it was all I could do to contain my excitement – you had me feeling like a boy feels when he has his first crush. You stole my heart when you agreed to have dinner with me and I knew I couldn't let you get away when you told me you fell for me even before I got the chance to tell you I love you..." Chandler turned to my father and spoke...

"Bazil... I am humbled, honored, and thankful that you gave me your blessing. In spite of everything you know of me and about me, you never need to be convinced of my love for your daughter. I promise you in front of God, these witnesses, and my future wife that I will be the best and only son-in-law and husband you could ever want for your daughter. I owe all my love for your daughter to you..." Chandler turned to my mother and spoke...

"Mary... From our very first date, Starr let me know how important you are in her life and that makes you a priority in mine. As much as I love her, she loves me – and I know you have everything to do with that. You encouraged your daughter to wait for the right man – and I thank God she listened to you and waited for me. I promise you in front of God, these witnesses, and my future wife that I will be the best and only son-in-law and husband you could ever want for your daughter. I owe all my love for your daughter to you as well..."

My father, my mother, and Beautiee remained standing as I began speaking my vows...

"Chandler..." I said as I took his hands... My mother always told me how important it was to stay focused and she was right - because ever since the first night I met you I've been focused on you. That night when you asked me to have coffee, God knew I needed you before I did. When you asked me to have dinner with you, you gave me something I was missing and I didn't realize it until that very moment – and I've been focused on you ever since. You've been teaching me lessons in love ever since you saw me – but the first lesson I learned was how to let you love me – and since I've learned that lesson – there's no turning back. When you asked me to have dinner with you – I knew you were going to be the one – and when I prayed and told God I needed you – his answer to my prayer was yes – and you were there – and now you're here... I turned to my mother and spoke...

"Mommy... You did it! You raised me to be everything I could be. When I called you to tell you I was in love with Chandler you cried and told me this is what you've always wanted for your baby – thank you for always wanting the best for me Mommy – I love you... I turned to my father and spoke...

"Daddy... As I got to know you, I knew you loved me but I had no idea how much you loved me until the night you gave Chandler your blessing to ask for my hand in marriage. You put your differences with my mother aside, you put my happiness first, and I'll always love you – you've kept every promise you've made to me..." Finally - I turned to Beautiee and spoke...

"Beautiee... You embraced me from the moment you laid eyes on me. When you introduced me to the people you work with, you introduced me as your daughter and that meant everything. You're fierce but you're also compassionate. I know why my father loves you – and I love you too. I've watched and admired how you love my father and I know my baby brother is going to be just fine...

"Chandler – put the ring on Starr's finger and repeat after me..." Darryl said...

"Okay – I'm ready..." Chandler said...

"Starr – I take you as my wife, with your faults and your strengths, as I offer myself to you with my faults and my strengths..." Chandler repeated after Darryl and then he continued... "I will help you when you need help and turn to you when I need help. Today - I choose to spend the rest of my life with you..." I started crying as Chandler repeated the vows to me. When he was finished, I took his face in my hands and kissed him...

"Starr – put the ring on Chandler's finger and repeat after me..."

"Okay – I'm ready..." I said...

"Chandler - I take you as my husband, with your faults and your strengths, as I offer myself to you with my faults and my strengths. I will help you when you need help and turn to you when I need help. Today – I choose to spend the rest of my life with you..."

"By the power invested in me by the State of Massachusetts and the City of Boston – I now pronounce you husband and wife - Chandler – you may kiss your bride! Ladies and Gentlemen – I present to you – Mr. & Mrs. Corbett!"

"Woo hoo!"

"Yeeaaa!" we heard as we held each other and continued kissing...

"I love you..." Beautiee said as she pulled my father into a kiss...

"I love you too..." my father breathed as he kissed her...

"I love you Troy..." Keisha said as she pulled Troy into a kiss...

"Keisha..." Troy cried as he kissed her...

"Charles..." Theresa cried as she pulled him into a kiss...

"Theresa..." Charles cried as he kissed her back. Smalls grabbed his wife, kissed her, and she kissed him back... and then...

"Oh my goodness!" my mother exclaimed as Darryl kissed her...

"Congratulations..." he said as he hugged her...

"Thank you..." she laughed...

"Congratulations Mary..." my father said as he hugged my mother...

"Thank you Bazil..." my mother said as she hugged him back...

"Congratulations Mary..." Beautiee said as she hugged my mother...

"Thank you Beautiee..." my mother said as she hugged her back...

"Congratulations..." my father said as he pulled us both into a hug...

"Stop crying..." Chandler laughed...

"I'll cry if I want to..." my father laughed...

"I know that's right!" Keisha said as she got up and pulled us both into a hug...

"I love you Keisha..." I said...

"We love you too..." Keisha said...

"Move Keisha!" Troy laughed as he pulled us away from her and into a hug...

"Damn – you too?" Chandler laughed...

"What?" Troy laughed as he wiped tears from his eyes...

"I love y'all..." Charles said as he grabbed us into a hug and started crying...

"We love you too..." Chandler said...

"I love y'all..." Theresa said as she pulled us into a hug and started crying...

"Theresa..." I cried...

"Congratulations..." Smalls said as he pulled us into a hug..."

"Thank you..." Chandler said...

"Congratulations..." Josefina said as she pulled us into a hug...

"Thank you..." I said...

"Congratulations..." Sam said as he pulled us both into a hug..."

"Thank you Sam..." Chandler said...

"Congratulations..." Joselyn said...

"Thank you Joselyn..." I said...

"Congratulations..." Sheila said...

"Thank you..." I said...

"Congratulations – I'm Sheila's husband, Henley..."

"Thank ya Henley – nice to meet you..."

"Nice to meet you too..."

"Ms. Crystal!" I said as I hugged her real tight..."

"Don't start Starr..." she laughed...

"I'm so happy you're here..."

"So am I... and I'm happy for you..."

"Thank you..."

"How soon will we get our marriage certificate?" I asked...

"You'll get it in about a week or so..."

"Thank you Darryl..." I said...

"Thank you Darryl..." Chandler said...

"You're welcome – now let's get started on your reception!" Darryl yelled as we all followed him into the banquet room...

Chapter 6

"Chandler..." I whispered as I heard 'You Are My Lady' playing...

"I love you Mrs. Corbett..." Chandler said as he pulled me into his arms and we danced...

"I love you too... Sergeant..." I whispered in his ear..."

"Now see... you in trouble..."

"I know..."

"You know what happens when you call me Sergeant..."

"Yes... I do..."

"I can't wait to get you upstairs..."

"Me either..."

"I'm gonna put it on you something fierce..."

"I know..." I breathed as Chandler held me tighter and I could feel his dick against me...

"You feel that?"

"Yeesss..."

"You want it?"

"Yeeess..." The song was over and we stood in the middle of the floor holding each other and kissing as everyone applauded...

"I love you...

47

"I love you too..." I breathed. Chandler pulled me into another kiss and held me as everyone applauded again. My father started tapping his champagne glass and everyone else did the same as we continued kissing...

"Come with me Mrs. Corbett..." Chandler said as he took my hand and led me to the head of the table, pulled out the chair, waited for me to sit down, and then sat down beside me. My father sat next to Chandler, my mother sat next to me, and then Beautiee sat next to my mother. Smalls, Josefina, Troy, Keisha, Charles, and Theresa sat at the table to the left of us and Sam, Joselyn, Sheila, Henley, and Ms. Crystal sat at the table to the right of us. A bottle of Prosecco was sitting in the middle of each table and the glasses were already filled. My father stood up and started crying. Chandler stood up beside him and started crying too...

"Chandler..." was all my father was able to get out. Chandler pulled my father into a hug and cried with him...

"Dad..." We all sat at the tables crying for a minute or so...

"Let me say this..." my father said as we all got quiet... "When I got arrested, I had no idea it was going to come to this..." my father said as we all bust out laughing...

"What's he talking about?" Charles whispered...

"Charles! Be quiet!" Theresa said...

"Neither did I..." Chandler laughed...

"Chandler is the Sergeant that works at the precinct where I was arrested...

"Oh shit!" Charles said...

"Charles! Shhh!" Theresa said...

"Lord... you got jokes..." my father said as we all laughed again...

"Oh shit!" Troy laughed...

"Chandler – even though I was guilty – you treated me with dignity and respect – and I'll never forget that..."

"Dad..." Chandler said as he started crying...

"Even after I knocked the shit outta you – you still respect me..." my father laughed...

"Daddy! You hit Chandler?" I gasped...

"You respected me enough to ask me for my blessing before you proposed to my daughter – and in that moment – I saw the man my daughter fell in love with – and I'm so proud to call you my son..."

"Dad..." Chandler cried...

"I love you son..." my father said as he cried with Chandler along with everybody else...

"Damn – I can't take it – I love y'all!" Smalls said as he got up and came over to hug my father...

"I love you too..." my father said. He waited for Smalls to sit down before he continued...

"Starr..." he said as he extended his hand to help me stand beside him...

"Yes Daddy?" I whispered as tears streamed down my face...

"I love you..." he said as he held my face and wiped my tears...

"I love you too Daddy..."

"I couldn't be more proud of you than I am right now...I'm just sorry I wasn't there for you sooner... please forgive me..." he cried...

"Please don't cry Daddy... I forgive you..." I cried as we hugged each other...

"Aww..." everyone said in unison...

"Starr..." my mother said as she stood up... "My beautiful baby girl..." she said as she teared up... "I love you..."

"I love you too Mommy..."

"I'm so proud of the woman you've become... and as much as I'd like to take all the credit... I can't... Chandler... thank you for loving my daughter..."

"Aww..." everyone said in unison...

"Beautiee..."

"Huh?" Beautiee answered in surprise as she turned to look at my mother...

"Thank you for everything you did for my daughter..."

"Is there a full moon or something?" Beautiee asked as everyone laughed...

"Beautiee – I mean it..."

"I know... I'm just playin'" Beautiee laughed...

"Starr..." Chandler said as he extended his hand to help me stand with him. I stood up and he pulled me into a kiss...

"Aww..." everyone said in unison...

"Okay – everyone raise your glass!" my father said... "To Mr. & Mrs. Corbett!" my father said as he took a sip of champagne...

"To Mr. & Mrs. Corbett!" everyone said in unison as they all took a sip of champagne...

"I have something I want to say..." I said as I remained standing... "Ms. Crystal – please stand up..."

"Starr... this isn't necessary..." she sighed as she stood up...

"Ms. Crystal – I know you were just doing your job – but you went above and beyond for me – you comforted me and you supported me – and I'll never forget that..."

"Dammit Starr – you gon' make me cry..." she said as I ran over to her and hugged her...

"Aww..." everyone said in unison...

"Alright – go on back over there with you're your husband..." she laughed...

"Okay – let's eat!" Chandler said...

"Chandler?"

"Yes Starr?"

"There's something we have to do first..."

"There is?"

"Yes..." I answered as Troy came over to the table, pulled my chair into the middle of the room, took me by the hand, and sat me down in the chair. Chandler stood there with a perplexed

51

look on his face so the men started chanting to help him out...

"Take it off! Take it off! Take it off!"

"Oooohhh!" Chandler laughed and then he came over to me and stood in front of me...

"Well?" I asked...

"Ssshhh..." Chandler said as he bent down to kiss me... and then he squatted down and pushed my legs open. Thank God my dress was long so nobody could see what was going on as he put his head up under my dress...

"Woo hoo!"

"Yea!"

"Take it off!" Chandler kissed his way up my thigh until he reached the garter and then he nibbled on my thigh as he took the garter in his teeth...

"Chandler... that tickles..." I laughed as I grabbed his head...

"Save it for later!" Theresa yelled out as everyone laughed and Chandler came out from under my dress with the garter in his teeth, stood up, and took a bow as everyone applauded. Chandler put the garter in his pocket, pulled me up out the chair, and kissed me hard...

"Woo hoo!"

"Yea!" My father came to get the chair and put it back at the table and waited for me to sit down before we all got ready to eat....

"I need everybody to hold hands..." Chandler said. Chandler waited for everyone to hold hands and then he stood up, took my hand,

and my father's hand... "Lord – thank you – for everything!"

"Amen!" we all said in unison. We all got up and went to the hors d'oeuvres station as jazz played in the background and I noticed Beautiee was still sitting at the table...

"Daddy – is Beautiee okay?"

"She's tired..."

"Daddy – something's wrong..."

"I know..."

"Watch her Daddy..."

"Starr – it's your wedding day..."

"But Daddy..."

"Chandler – help me..."

"Mmmm..." I moaned as Chandler pulled me into a kiss...

"Okay..." I sighed as we got the following hors d'oeuvrs:

Spinach Dip
Marinated Olives
Antipasto Platter,
Assorted Mini Deep Dish Pizzetta
Assorted Miniature Calzones

My father made a plate for Beautiee and took it to the table. We all sat down to eat and I tried to leave it alone but I couldn't...

"Beautiee?"

"Yes Starr?"

"Are you okay?"

"The baby's coming..."

"Oh my God! Daddy..."

"Starr?"

"Yes Beautiee?"

"Relax..."

"I can't – Daddy..."

"Starr?"

"Yes Beautiee?"

"What did I say?"

"Okay Beautiee..." I sighed...

"Beautiee... are you sure you're okay?" my mother asked...

"I'm having a baby..." Beautiee answered as she ate... "I was starving!"

"I'm glad you're eating..." my father said...

"Your son has a very healthy appetite..." she laughed and I started to feel better...

"You alright?" Chandler asked...

"Yea..." I sighed...

"You ready?"

"Yea..."

"I'm so happy for them..." Smalls said...

"So am I..." Josefina agreed...

"Who'da thought Chandler would end up being his son-in-law?" Troy said...

"I know – right?" Keisha agreed...

"I can't believe Bazil knocked the shit outta Chandler and they're still cool!" Charles laughed...

"Oh so you don't remember what happened between you and my father?" Theresa asked...

"Hell yea I remember – I ran!" Charles laughed along with everyone else at the table...

"I can't believe she invited her worker from Section 8..." Theresa said...

"Right – I wouldn't've invited my worker to a mutha fuckin' thing – nasty Bitch!" Keisha said as everyone laughed...

"Sam... look at them..." Joselyn said...

"Reminds you of us... don't they?" Sam asked...

"Yea..." Joselyn said as Sam kissed her...

"Y'all still ain't give us no grandbabies!" Henley said...

"Oh my God – Mommy!" Joselyn laughed...

"Uh uh – I'm the one talkin' to you!" Henley snapped...

"Yes sir – we gon' get right on that – tonight!" Sam laughed...

"Yea, yea – that's what what you told me last week!" Sheila laughed...

"I bet you won't have to tell them to work on grandkids..." Crystal said as everyone at the table laughed...

"It was so nice of Starr to invite you to the wedding!" Joselyn said...

"I told her she didn't have to – but she wasn't trying to hear it..."

"Well it's nice meeting you..." Sheila said...

"Nice meeting you all too... I'm so happy for them..." Crystal said...

I noticed Beautiee got up from the table and my father followed her...

"Beautiee? Are you okay?"

"No..." she answered as my father followed her into the bathroom and shut the door...

"What's wrong?" he asked as he teared up...

"We're having a baby..."

"Oh my God!"

"Bazil... shhh!"

"I love you so much!" he said as he kissed her hard...

"I love you too... but I need you to keep this between us..."

"That's gonna be hard..."

"Bazil!"

"Okay, okay... I won't say anything..." he said as he held her...

"I'm in labor..."

"Le'me go get Keisha..."

"Bazil!"

"Okay, okay – I'll do whatever you want..."

"Thank you – now help me sit on this toilet... oh shit..."

"Beautiee – what happened?"

"My water just broke..."

"Okay – what do I do?"

"I'm going to go change..."

"You stay here – I'll bring you something – I'll be right back..." he said as he ran upstairs...

"Keisha – where you goin'?"

"To the bathroom – I'll be right back..." she said as she jumped up from the table and ran to the bathroom... "Beautiee – you in there?"

"Yea..."

"Open the door!"

"Alright..." Beautiee said as she opened the door...

"Oh shit – your water broke?"

"Yea..."

"Where's Bazil?"

"I'm right here..." he said as he came in the bathroom...

"We need to get you to the hospital..."

"Keisha... please..."

"Whatchu need?"

"Go back to the table... with your husband... I'll be fine..."

"You sure?"

"Yes... I'll be out in a minute..."

"Okay – but if I don't see you – I'm comin' back..."

"Okay – now go before people start wondering if there's a party in here..." Beautiee laughed...

"Here – let me help you..." Bazil said as he helped her put on another outfit...

"Thank you..."

"You sure you're okay?"

"Bazil!"

"Okay, okay – c'mon..." he said a she walked Beautiee back into the banquet room...

"There you are! Is everything alright?" I asked...

"Yes Starr – I just went to pee..." I answered as everyone laughed...

"Well you're just in time for the next course..." I said as I got up and everyone else followed. We all went over to the Italian Family Style Station and saw the following:

Roasted Veal Parmesan with
Mariana Sauce over Linguini
Sautéed Chicken Piccata over
Angel Hair Pasta
Shrimp Scampi over
Angel Hair Pasta
Meatballs with Bolognese Sauce
Over Spaghetti

Oven-Roasted Potatoes
Charcoal Grilled Vegetables
Caesar Salad
Caprese Flatbread
Breadsticks
Garlic Bread with Butter

"Daddy – that's a lot of food!" I laughed...

"You'll see how your appetite changes once you're pregnant..." my mother laughed as we all went back to the table...

"Oh my God – that looks so good – thank you!" Beautiee said as she started eating...

"You're welcome..." my father said as he kissed her...

"Bazil?"

"Yes Beautiee..."

"I love you — but I can't eat if you keep kissing me..." she laughed. Everyone continued eating until they were finished and then it was time for cake...

"Starr?"

"Yes Chandler?"

"Come with me..." he said as he stood up and extended his hand...

"Okay!" I squealed as he took me over to the cake...

"Smash it in his face! Smash it in his face!" everyone yelled...

"Chandler... I don't wanna..."

"Too late!" Chandler laughed as he took some of the cake off his plate and smashed it in my face as everyone laughed...

"Chandler... you got it in my hair!"

"I'm sorry..." he sighed...

"I'm not!" I laughed as I took a piece of cake and smashed it on the side of his face, making sure I got some of the cake and icing in his hair as everyone laughed...

"Come here Starr..." he said as he smiled at me mischievously...

"No..." I laughed...

"I said..." he laughed as he pulled me close to him... "Come here... and open your mouth..."

he laughed as he held a small piece of cake in between his fingers...

"Okay... okay..." I laughed as I opened my mouth and he put the cake in my mouth... "Mmmm... it's good... your turn..." I said as I picked up a small piece of cake in between my fingers and held it in front of his mouth...

"Okay... I'ma open my mouth... and you not gonna smash it on my nose... right?"

"Chandler!"

"Okay..." he laughed as he opened his mouth and I put a piece of cake in his mouth...

"Mmmm..." he said as he pulled me into a kiss and put his tongue in my mouth with cake on it...

"Mmmm..." I moaned...

"Y'all need us to leave?" Troy asked as everyone laughed...

"Y'all can stay if y'all want..." Chandler laughed as he picked up another piece of cake, held it between his lips, and pulled me into another kiss...

"Aww shit!"

"Woo hoo!"

"C'mon – let's let everyone get a piece of cake..." Chandler laughed as we went back to the table...

"I've never had cake like that before..." I laughed...

"Me either..."

"I wanna do it again..."

"We can..." My father came back to the table with some cake for Beautiee and I noticed her wincing in pain...

"You okay?" my father whispered in her ear...

"Yea... I just have a little indigestion..." she lied...

"You just had a contraction... didn't you?"

"Bazil... could you get me some coffee?"

"Sure..." my father said as he got up...

"Beautiee... you don't like the cake?" Chandler asked...

"It's good – I just have a little indigestion..."

"Here..." my father said as he put a cup of coffee on the table for Beautiee...

"Oh God... I'm gonna be sick!" she said as she jumped up and ran towards the bathroom and my father was right behind her...

"Uuuuggghhh!" Beautiee grunted as she hurled up everything she ate into the toilet...

"Beautiee..." my father sighed as he teared up...

"Bazil... I'm fine..."

"No you're not!"

"Bazil... I'm fine..." she sighed as she hugged him...

"You promise?"

"I'd be better if you take that washcloth and run it in some water for me..."

"Okay..." he said as he put the washcloth in warm water...

"Beautiee – you alright?"

"Yes Keisha… I'm alright…"

"No she isn't…"

"Bazil!"

"Beautiee… what's going on?"

"I threw up…"

"That's all?"

"I'm in labor…"

"Beautiee! Why didn't you tell me?"

"Because you and Bazil both want me to go to the hospital – and I don't want to make this day about me – it's Starr's wedding day!"

"Beautiee – I think she'll understand…"

"Keisha… No…"

"Okay… but I still think you should go…"

"Bazil will make sure I'm fine…"

"You right – Bazil – you better…"

"I will Keisha…"

"Keisha – please don't tell Troy…"

"Beautiee – you already know…"

"Okay – can you at least wait until y'all get home?"

"Sure… I can do that…"

"Thank you…" she said as she hugged her…

"I love you…"

"I love you too…"

"I'ma go upstairs and lay down – if I go back in there Starr won't leave me alone…" she laughed…

"You right…" Keisha laughed…

"I'ma make sure you get upstairs – then I'll go say goodnight to everybody..."

"Okay..." Beautiee breathed as another contraction hit...

"C'mon – let's get you upstairs..." he said as he took her upstairs. When he came back into the banquet room and I didn't see Beautiee, I knew something was wrong...

"Daddy? Where's Beautiee?"

"She went to lay down..."

"Is she okay Daddy?"

"She's having a baby Starr..."

"She got sick..."

"That happens when you're pregnant honey..." my mother said... "Especially when you eat spicy food...

"May I have everyone's attention?" my father asked as he stood up and we all got quiet...

"Thank you all for coming. Please stay as long as you like. My wife had some indigestion and she's feeling nauseous so she went to lay down. I'm going to go make sure she's okay. Good night..." he said as he left...

"Beautiee..."

"Yes Bazil?"

"How are you feeling?"

"Tired..." Bazil got in bed behind her and spooned her...

"Did everyone leave?"

"They're still downstairs..."

"What did you tell them?"

"I told them you had indigestion and you were feeling nauseous so you came to lay down and I was coming to make sure you were okay..."

"I love you Bazil..." she yawned...

"I love you too..." Bazil yawned as they both went to sleep...

Chapter 7

"Starr... my beautiful wife..." Chandler said as he took me by the hand and led me towards the bed...

"Yes Chandler... my husband..."

"Sit down... I have something for you..." Chandler said as he sat down beside me, opened the laptop, and started playing the video...

"Oh my God – that was the first time..." I cried as I watched myself...

"Yes..."

"You recorded us..."

"Yes..."

"I'm so embarrassed..."

"Why?"

"I was naive..."

"No... you were beautiful..."

"I didn't know what do..."

"You did everything right..." Chandler said as he wiped my tears...

"Look... you're signing to me..." I whispered as I continued to cry..."

"You're crying..."

"I was happy..."

"And you're happy now..."

"Yes..."

"Look..." Chandler said as he pointed to the laptop and I watched him kissing my tattoo, starting at the bottom of my feet...

"It felt so good..."

"I couldn't wait to taste you..."

"Oh Chandler... I peed..." I laughed as I continued watching...'

"You gave me a golden shower...

"You didn't mind..."

"I released your inhibitions..."

"Yes... you did..."

"You gave yourself to me..." he said as I watched him get on top of me and start making love to me...

"You made me feel loved..."

"You are loved... and right there... you're loving me..." he said as he pointed to the laptop... "You look so beautiful when you're having an orgasm... I love that look on your face... you're glowing..." he said as he pointed to the laptop and I saw myself... and Chandler was right... I was glowing...

"I love you... my husband..."

"I love you... my wife..."

"I love how you make me feel..."

"I know..."

"I love how you make me look..."

"I love making you look that way..."

"I love making love to you..."

"I know..."

"I want to make love to you... and I want to see it..."

"You want me to record it?"

"Yes... I want to see me... loving you..."

"Okay..." Chandler said as he lay back on the bed...

"Move up to the headboard..."

"Okay..."

"Sit back..."

"Okay..."

"Get your phone..." Chandler picked up his phone, hit record, and watched me as I got down between his legs, unzipped his pants, and took out his dick...

"Starr..." I began kissing the sides of his dick as I stroked it with my hand...

"Starr..." I looked up at Chandler to make sure he was recording and I took his dick in my mouth...

"Starr..." I took him all the way in my mouth down to his balls, I looked up at him to make sure he was recording, and I started sucking him fiercely...

"Starr... you... I'ma... drop... the... phone..."

"Mmmm.... Mmmm...." I moaned with his dick in my mouth... I knew it was torture for him to hold the phone when he wanted to grab my head and fuck my mouth... and I loved it...

"Starr... I'm... I'm..."

"I know..." I said as I stroked his dick while sucking the head...

"Stttaaarrrrr!" Chandler moaned as his sperm shot up out his dick, down the back of my throat, and dribbled out my mouth down his dick as I continued sucking... and Chandler recorded it all... "Please..."

"Yes Chandler..."

"Let me fuck you..."

"Put the phone here..." I said as I pointed to the night stand. Chandler positioned the phone on the nightstand to make sure I could be seen clearly... and once he knew the camera was in position, he grabbed my head and started fucking my mouth...

"That's it Starr... suck it..." he moaned as he held my head with both hands and continued fucking my mouth...

"Mmmm... mmm... I moaned on his dick so he could feel the vibration...

"Shit... Fuck... I'm coming! Aaahhhh!" Chandler moaned as he came in my mouth... and I swallowed... and sucked... "Starr..."

"Yes... my husband..."

"Come here..." he said as he pulled me up... "I love you..." he said as he held my face and kissed me...

"I love you too... my husband..."

"Let me help you out of your dress..."

"Okay..."

"Go stand in front of the mirror..."

"Okay..." Chandler brought the phone over to where I was standing. He untied the sash and recorded us as he stood behind me touching me, kissing my neck, and squeezing my breasts.

I closed my eyes as Chandler held me close to him and kissed me on my neck and shoulders...

"Open your eyes... look at what I'm doing to you..."

"Okay..." I breathed as I opened my eyes and watched him kiss my neck and shoulders. Now that I was watching... as well as feeling... I was so turned on... "Take me..." I breathed... Chandler took me by the hand, led me to the bed, laid me down, gave me the phone so I could record him, and stood there in front of me, undressing himself. When he was completely nude, he stood there and smiled as I looked back at him. Chandler knew I wanted him and he enjoyed making me want, making me wait... "Please..."

"Please what?"

"Please... make love to me..." Chandler climbed upon the bed, put the phone on the night stand to make sure we were in view, spread my legs, lowered himself down to my pussy, spread my lips, and started sucking my clit... "Chandlllleeerrr!" I moaned as he deliberately held me in place so I couldn't move... "Ohhh... Ooohhh... Ooohhh..."

"Mmmm... you taste so good..."

"Chandler... Chandler... Chandler..." I moaned as he pushed my legs further apart and put his tongue inside me... "I'm cumming... I'm cumming..." I moaned as my legs shook around his head...

"Now..." Chandler said as he came up between my legs... "I'll take you..." he said as he eased himself inside me...

"Oh... Chandler..." I moaned as he took my breast in his mouth while thrusting inside me..."

"Mmmm.... Yes..." he moaned while sucking my breast..."

"Chandler..." I moaned as he started thrusting harder...

"Fuck... Starr..." he breathed in my ear as he picked up my legs, got up on his knees, and thrust harder and deeper...

"Chandler... Ohhh... Chandler..." Chandler laid down on top of me, wrapped his arms underneath the small of my back, and I wrapped my legs around him and locked my ankles so he couldn't move...

"Ummph... Ummph... Ummph..."

"Huuh... Huuh... Huuh..."

"Fuck... Ummph..."

"I'm cumming Chandler..."

"Cum for me..."

"Huuh... Huuh... Huuh... Huuuuuuh!"

"Uugh! Uugh! Uugh! Uuuugggghhhh!" Chandler stayed inside me, put his tongue in my mouth, and we tongued each other down for a few moments until I heard Beautiee...

"Fuck! Bazil! I'm coming!"

"Damn..." Chandler laughed... "Your father's up there putting it on her... and I'm down here... putting it on you..." he said as he kissed me again... and I heard Beautiee again...

"Fuck! Bazil! I'm coming!"

"Sounds like your father's the man..." Chandler laughed...

"Something's wrong..."

"What?"

"Chandler – something's wrong – we gotta go..."

"Starr – it's our wedding night..."

"Chandler!"

"Okay Starr – I'm comning..." Chandler said as he got up off the bed and threw on his robe. I threw on my pajamas, threw on my robe, and we ran out our room to my mother's room...

"Starr – what are you doing?"

"Mommy!" I yelled as I banged on the door...

"Starr?"

"Mommy – open the door – Beautiee needs our help!"

"Hang on Starr – I'm coming!" she said as she jumped up, opened the door... and we saw Thompson...

"Jermoll..." Chandler said...

"Chandler..."

"You? And Mary?"

"Me... and Mary..."

"Mommy! C'mon!" I yelled as we ran upstairs... "Daddy! Open the door!" I yelled as I banged on the door and my father opened the door...

"Oh my God – Beautiee's in labor..." my mother said as she went over to the bed and started rubbing Beautiee's back...

"I don't know what to do..." my father said...

"You're doing fine Bazil – take her hand..." my mother said...

"Starr!"

"Yes Beautiee?"

"Get my phone!"

"Okay..." I said as I hurried up to get her phone and tried to give it to her...

"I want you to record... Uggghhh!" she yelled as another labor pain hit her...

"Breathe Beautiee..." my mother said as she continued rubbing Beautiee's back...

"Starr ... the baby's coming... I want you to record it!"

"Oh hell no – I'on wanna see that!" Chandler said...

"Oh God – it hurts – please help me!" Beautiee cried...

"I'm here... relax... your son is okay..." God said...

"I love you Beautiee..." my father said as he kissed her... and another labor pain hit...

"I love you too... Uggghhh!" she yelled...

"Starr!" my mother yelled as she pulled back the sheet... "She's ready... start recording..."

"Okay Mommy!" I said as I started recording. Chandler couldn't see anything if he

72

wanted to – which he didn't – because I was standing directly in front of her... "Oh my God! I see his head!" I squealed...

"Bazil! Get down there and help your son come into the world!" my mother commanded... "Okay Beautiee – push!"

"Uggghhh!"

"Oh my God... Beautiee... our son... he's coming..." my father cried...

"Push!" my mother commanded...

"Uggghhh!"

"He's here!" my father cried as he pulled him out and held him...

"Mary... my purse... get the scissors..."

"Okay..."

"Starr... keep recording..."

"Okay..."

"Give the scissors to Bazil..."

"Okay..." my mother said as she turned the handle to Bazil..."

"What?" my father asked...

"Cut the cord Daddy..." Beautiee said...

"I won't hurt him?"

"No... you won't hurt him..." Beautiee answered...

"You promise?"

"I promise..."

"Okay..." my father said as he cut the cord... "Hello son..." my father cried as he held him...

"Let me see him..." Beautiee said...

"Here…" my father said as he handed my lil' brother to Beautiee…

"Hello Jay… it's nice to finally meet you…"

"Chandler… look…" I said…

"Is she decent?"

"Yes Chandler… I'm decent…" Beautiee laughed…

"Oh wow… he looks just like his father… congratulations…"

"Thank you…" my father breathed…

"Is everything okay in there? Our other guests have complained about the commotion…" Darrly said…

"C'mon in Darryl…" Beautiee said…

"Oh my goodness – you had the baby – we've never had that happen here – congratulations!"

"Thank you Darryl…" my father said…

"Do you need a doctor?"

"Yes Darryl…"

"I'll get an ambulance – I'm so happy…" Darryl said as he hurried off to call the ambulance…

"I'm coming with you…" I said…

"Excuse me?" Chandler interrupted…

"Starr… you're going back to your room… with your husband…" my mother said…

"Beautiee…"

"Starr…" Beautiee interrupted… "It's your wedding night…"

"But…"

"Starr... I'll take it from here..." my father laughed... "You belong to Chandler now..."

"Yes... you belong to me..." Chandler said as he took the phone from me, gave it to Beautiee, and took my hand...

"Can I stay here until the ambulance comes?"

"Yes Starr..." Chandler said as he pulled me into a kiss...

"Beautiee?"

"Yes Darryl?"

"They're here..." Darryl said as he brought them in...

"Can you get up on the stretcher?" the technician asked...

"Yes..." Beautiee said as she gave my lil' brother to my father and she got up on the stretcher...

"I'm coming with you..." my father said...

"Of course..." Beautiee laughed... "Give me the baby... and get the phone... I need pictures..."

"Okay..." my father beamed as they secured Beautiee on the stretcher and took her downstairs to the ambulance...

"Mary..." my father called to my mother as she started to leave the room...

"Yes Bazil?" My father pulled my mother into a kiss. Chandler looked at him and then we looked at each other...

"Thank you..."

"You're welcome Bazil..."

"Starr..."

"Yes Daddy?"

"Come here..." he said as he pulled me into a hug and held me... "I love you..."

"I love you too Daddy..."

"You're going to make Chandler very happy..."

"I know..." I laughed...

"Chandler..." my father said as he pulled him into a hug...

"Yes Bazil?"

"I love you too..." my father said and then he left to go join Beautiee in the ambulance.

Chapter 8

"Come here Mrs. Corbett..." Chandler said as he closed the door, took me by the hand, and led me to the bed. I stood still as Chandler took his time taking off my robe, kissing me on my neck and shoulders as he did so...

"Mmmm... Mr. Corbett... I moaned as Chandler unbuttoned my pajama top, slid it off, and began sucking on my breasts... "Oh... Mr. Corbett..."

"Yes Mrs. Corbett?' Chandler answered as he pulled me close to him, held me, and began massaging my back. I looked him in his eyes as I slid his robe off him and felt his dick pressing against me...

"Well well well..." I said as I started stroking his dick... "What are we going to do with this?"

"I have an idea..." Chandler said as he pushed me down on the bed onto my back...

"Okay..." I watched Chandler put the phone up on the tall dresser, hit the record button, and position it so it would record us on the bed...

"Spread your legs..." Chandler said as he climbed on top of me and positioned himself so his dick was near my mouth and his head was down between my legs... "Take my dick in your mouth..." Chandler said and then he started kissing my pussy. It was a little awkward at first but once I got the hang of it – it felt good – especially with Chandler licking and sucking my pussy... "Hmmmph... Hmmmph... Hmmmph... Hmmmph..."

"Ummmph... Ummmph... Ummmph... Ummmph..."

"Hmmmph... Hmmmph... Hmmmph... Hmmmph...

"Ummmph... Ummmph... Ummmph... Ummmph..." Chandler's dick was so hard in my mouth... I was enjoying what I was doing... I was enjoying what he was doing... and then... just as I was about ready to come... Chandler flipped us over... he was on the bottom... I was on top... and as Chandler spread my legs around his face and sucked my pussy harder... I took his dick in my mouth further... and our bodies shook as we both came simultaneously...

"Hmmmph... Hmmmph... Hmmmph... Hmmmph!"

"Ummmph... Ummmph... Ummmph... Ummmph!"

"Hmmmph... Hmmmph... Hmmmph... Hmmmph!

"Ummmph... Ummmph... Ummmph... Ummmph!" I swallowed every bit of him and then I turned myself around and pulled him into a kiss before he could say anything...

"Mmmm..." I moaned as I put my tongue in Chandler's mouth and tasted myself. I stopped kissing Chandler, held his face, and smiled as I wiped my juices off his chin...

"Stop that..." Chandler said as he kissed me...

"Your face... it's..."

"It's wet... from my wife..."

"It's soaked..."

"You came hard..."

"Speaking of hard..." I said as we continued kissing...

"I was..."

"You were..."

"I loved it..."

"I did too..."

"What did you love?"

"I loved how you felt... in my mouth..."

"I loved that too..."

"I loved how your mouth felt on me..."

"I loved that too..."

"I've never done that before..."

"I know..."

"I..." I said as I kissed him... "wanna... do... that... again..."

"I know..."

"Can we?"

"Of course..."

"I can't wait until we get to Bermuda..."

"Me either..." Chandler said as we lay together holding each other...

"I wanna make love to you in our suite..."

"Me too..."

"I wanna make love to you... on the private balcony... under the purple sun... set..." I yawned...

"Me... too..." Chandler yawned as we both fell asleep.

Chapter 9

"You're awake..." Bazil said. Beautiee opened her eyes and smiled as she watched Bazil holding Jay... "He's hungry..."

"So feed him..."

"I don't have a bottle..." Bazil laughed...

"Give me the baby..."

"Okay..." Bazil said as he handed Jay to her...

"Now... come in back of me... and hold me..."

"Okay..." Bazil said as he got into bed with Beautiee, got behind her, and held her...

"Now... take my breast... put it in his mouth... and feed your son..." Bazil did as Beautiee told him and watched as his son latched on to her breast and eat...

"I love you..." he breathed as he kissed her neck..."

"I love you too..."

"Are you in pain?"

"No..."

"I miss you..."

"I miss you too..."

"How soon can we make love again?"

"We can make love anytime you want – but when we get home... I don't wanna make love..."

"You don't? Why?"

"For months – I've shared your body with our son..."

"I know..."

"When we get home – I want to fuck you..."

"Oh... I see..." Bazil laughed...

"I want to feel you like I did on our wedding night..."

"I love the sound of that..." he said as he held her and kissed her neck and shoulders...

"I loved the feel of it..."

"So did I..."

'I want to wrap myself around you and feel you loving me... without our son in between us..."

"So do I..."

"I want to ride your face and watch you pleasure me without our son blocking my view..."

"I can't wait for you to come home..." Bazil breathed in her ear...

"I want to lie on my back and take your dick in my mouth as you lay on top of me, spread my legs, and take my pussy in your mouth... it's been so long..."

"You will... I promise..."

"I want to come hard in your mouth while I'm holding your ass and pushing your dick into my mouth... and I want to feel your stomach on mine and feel your body shake uncontrollably as I suck the life outtta you... swallow it... and hold

82

you on top of me... in my mouth... until I want to let go... if I want to let go... and if I don't let go... I want you to flip me over... hold me down on top of you... and lick and suck me simultaneously as I'm stroking and sucking you... until you feel me trembling against your body... without our son in between us..."

"Yes Beautiee... yes..."

"Mr. Osgood – Mrs. Osgood – I have wonderful news..." the doctor said as he came in...

"Yes Doctor?" Bazil asked...

"Your son is doing well – you can go home today..." Bazil looked at Beautiee and smiled mischievously...

"How soon can we start having sex doctor?"

"I normally tell my patients to wait six weeks to give their body time to adjust and get back to normal – but some of my patients get pregnant again before they leave the hospital..." he laughed...

"Damn!" Bazil laughed...

"It's really up to you – if you feel up to it – but ideally you should wait 6 weeks..."

"Okay – thank you doctor..."

Chapter 10

"I love you Jermoll..." Mary said as they held each other...

"I love you too Mary..."

"I had no idea..." Mary whispered as she started crying...

"Why? Don't you believe you deserve love?" Jermoll asked as he held her and kissed her...

"No..."

"Then why were you with me?"

"You made me feel beautiful..."

"You are beautiful Mary..."

"Why the others?"

"I did that... because I could..."

"What changed?" Jermoll sat up in the bed beside Mary...

"If I tell you – it stays between us..."

"It will – I promise..." Mary said as she sat up in the bed next to Jermoll...

"When Beautiee was arrested..."

"Jermoll... no..."

"Yes..."

"Does Bazil know?"

"Yes..."

"And you're alive?"

"I didn't hurt her..."

"But you were going to?"

"I didn't know who she was... until she told me... I swear..."

"Did Bazil believe you?"

"It didn't matter..."

"Oh my God... what happened?"

"He took my manhood..." Jermoll whispered...

"He raped you?"

"No..."

"Oh thank God..."

"The only reason he didn't rip my dick off when he had it in his hands was because I didn't rape his wife..."

"Does Chandler know?"

"No..."

"Can you trust Bazil not to tell him?"

"Yes..."

"How can you be sure?"

"Because he's happy..."

"You're right... he's happy..."

"We can be happy to Mary..."

"Can we?"

"Yes..."

"How?"

"I'll go see Conrad... I'll pay him... you'll be free... we can get married... and I can take care of you... like you've been taking care of me..." Jermoll said as he kissed her...

"Jermoll..."

"Say yes... please..."

"Yes Jermoll... I'll marry you..."

"Okay...." Jermoll said as he got out of the bed and started getting dressed...

"Where are you going?"

"I'm going to set you free..." Jermoll said as he kissed her goodbye and left...

"Hello —may I help you?" Dominique asked as Jermoll walked into the Cox Law Firm...

"I'm here to see Attorney Cox..."

"May I tell him your name?"

"Thompson..."

"Please have a seat..." Dominique said as she called Conrad on the intercom...

"Yes Dominique?"

"There's a Mr. Thompson here to see you..."

"I'm not expecting anyone by that name..."

"Mr. Thompson?"

"Yes Maam?"

"Please call me Dominique - my mother is Maam..." she laughed...

"Yes Dominique?"

"I'm sorry but Mr. Cox isn't expecting you today..."

"He's expecting Mary..."

"Hold on a moment... Mr. Cox?"

"Yes Dominique?"

"Mr. Thompson asked me to tell you you're expecting Mary..."

"Did he?"

"Yes sir...."

"Send him in...

"Yes sir... Mr. Thompson?"

"Yes Dominique?"

"Mr. Cox will see you..."

"Thank you..." Jermoll said as he got up and went into Conrad's office...

"Officer Thompson – what can I do for you?" Conrad asked with a smile...

"You can give me a receipt..."

"I beg your pardon?"

"Please give me a receipt... for $50,000... for Mary..."

"I see..." Conrad said as he smiled... "Dominique?"

"Yes Mr. Cox?"

"Please prepare the paperwork for Mary Smith... and give a copy to Mr. Thompson..."

"Yes Mr. Cox..."

"I'll give you a receipt for payment... as soon as I see my money..." Conrad said as he smiled...

"Here..." Jermoll said as he placed a duffel bag on the table. Conrad opened the duffel bag, smelled the money, and smiled...

"It's all there..." Jermoll said...

"I know..."

"Mary's free now..."

"Yes... she is..."

"Here's a copy of the paperwork..." Dominique said as she brought in a manila envelope with documents...

"Thank you..." Jermoll said as he took the envelope...

"I'll have the documents filed later today – Mr. Osgood's attorney will be notified immediately..." Conrad said...

"Thank you..."

"You're welcome... have a good day..."

"You do the same..." Jermoll said as he left Conrad's office and left the law firm...

"Conrad speaking..." Conrad said as he answered his cell phone...

"I received the documents..."

"Good..."

"She really came through with the money..."

"Yes she did..."

"Oh well – congratulations..."

"Thank you..."

"I'll be by later today to pick up my payment..."

"I'll come to you..."

"The usual spot?"

"Yes..."

"Later..."

"Later..." Conrad said as he hung up...

"Attorney Smalls' office – this is Valarie..."

"Good morning Valarie – this is Conrad..."

"Good morning Conrad – I'll put you right through to Smalls – hold on please... Smalls?"

"Yes Valarie?"

"I have Conrad on the phone for you..."

"Thank you Valarie... Conrad – what else can I do for you?"

"It's done..."

"It's done?"

"She withdrew..."

"When will I get confirmation?"

"It's being filed as we speak..."

"Thank you..."

"You're welcome..." Conrad said as he hung up...

"Good morning..." Bazil answered...

"It's over..."

"I don't understand..."

"She withdrew the lawsuit..."

"Thank you..." Bazil whispered...

"You're welcome..."

"When will I get confirmation?"

"It's being filed as we speak..."

"I love you..."

"I love you too..." Smalls said as he hung up...

"Mmmm....." Beautiee moaned as Bazil kissed her awake...

"It's over..."

"What?" Beautiee asked as she sat up in bed...

"It's over..." Bazil said as he smiled...

"She fixed it?"

"She fixed it..."

"Oh thank God!" Beautiee breathed...

"You're welcome..." God said...

"Now... we can get back to business..." Bazil said as he climbed in bed beside her, pulled her down onto her back, lay down on top of her, kissed her deeply... and Jay started crying...

Chapter 11

"Good morning Chandler..." Bazil answered...

"Are you up for company?"

"If you need us to be..."

"Who is it?" Beautiee yawned...

"It's Chandler..."

"Is everything alright?"

"He wants to know if we're up for company..." Bazil laughed...

"Give me about an hour..."

"Chandler... Beautiee says..."

"I heard..." Chandler laughed...

"We'll see you soon..." Bazil said as he hung up... "Might as well get up..." Bazil said but Beautiee stopped him...

"What's wrong?"

"I'm horny..." Beautiee said as she pulled him into a kiss...

"Are you sure this is a good idea?"

"Only one way to find out..." Beautiee said as she pulled Bazil on top of her..."

"I don't want to hurt you..."

"I won't let you hurt me... don't worry..."

"What if you get pregnant again?"

"What if I do?"

"You'd have another baby? For me?"

"Yes Bazil... I'd have another baby... for you..."

"I love you so much..."

"I love you too..."

"Okay... if I'm hurting you..."

"Hurry up before Jay wakes up..." Beautiee breathed...

"Okay..." Bazil breathed as he eased himself inside her...

"Mmmm..." Beautiee moaned...

"Damn... what the fuck did my son do?" Bazil breathed as he started thrusting...

"Bazil... oh shit... fuck..."

"You're ready to come... aren't you?"

"Yes Bazil... yes..."

"Can I go harder?"

"Yes..."

"Uuugh! Uuugh! Uuugh! Uuugh!

"Huuhh! Huuhh! Huuhh! Huuhh!

"Damn your pussy feels so fuckin' good..."

"So... does... your... dick... Aaahhhhh!"

"Uuuugggghhhh!!!" Bazil continued to lay on top of Beautiee, inside Beautiee, kissing her deeply...

"Thank you... I needed.... that..."

"So... did... I..."

"Can... we... just... stay... here... in... bed?"

"We... have... company... coming..."

"They... just... wanna... see... Jay..."

"So... you... wanna... stay... in... bed?"

"Not... without... you..."

"Okay... I'm getting... up..."

"I... need... more..."

"Me... too..."

"Okay... I'll get the baby... you make coffee..."

"I'm coming with you..."

"You... always... do..."

"Yes... I... do..." Bazil got up, helped Beautiee up, and they went to wake up Jay... "Well look at you!" Bazil smiled as he picked up his son. Beautiee watched as Jay smiled and cooed with his father and she smiled too. "You wanna hold him?"

"In a minute – he's so happy with you right now..."

"Okay – I'll take him downstairs..." Bazil said as Beautiee followed them back to the bedroom. Bazil handed Jay to Beautiee to put on his robe and slippers and Jay started squirming...

"Hold on Jay – you can go back to Daddy in a minute..." Beautiee laughed...

"Come here son..." Bazil said as he held out his arms...

"Oh my God – look at him!" Beautiee laughed as she watched Jay moving his arms and legs to go be with Bazil...

"I gotchu..." Bazil said as he took Jay from Beautiee...

"I'ma remember that when your lil' ass is hungry..." Beautiee laughed as she put on her robe and slippers and followed Bazil and Jay downstairs....

"I'm surprised he's not hungry yet..." Bazil said...

"He'll be hungry in a while – besides – I need a break from poppin' my titty out..." Beautiee laughed...

"Can I have some milk? Please?" Bazil asked...

"Yes Bazil... I have enough for both of you..." Beautiee laughed as they went into the kitchen...

"Can I ask you something?"

"Yes Bazil..."

"Does it turn you on?"

"What?"

"When Jay..."

"No Bazil... it's different..."

"Oh so when I do it... you like it..."

"Yes..."

"Does it hurt?"

"Sometimes I get sore..."

"I'm sorry..."

"Not from you Bazil..."

"Oh... the baby?"

"Yea..."

"Can you fix it?" he asked as he held Jay with one arm and made coffee with the other...

94

"I can put cream around the nipple – but I can't put cream on the nipple – we don't want the baby to eat it..."

"How long can you breast feed?"

"As long as I can tolerate it – 6 months is good – a year is better – but I'm shuttin' it down as soon as he gets teeth in his mouth..." Beautiee laughed...

"Does that mean you'll shut me down too?" he asked as he handed Jay to her...

"You don't use your teeth... and when you do... it tickles..."

"Like this?" Bazil asked as he put the coffee on the table, leaned forward, and began nibbling on Beautiee's neck...

"Yes..." Beautiee laughed... and Jay laughed too... "Do it again!" Beautiee squealed...

"Like this?" Bazil asked as he leaned forward and nibbled on Beautiee's neck again... this time adding a growling sound... and Jay laughed... "You like what I'm doing to Mommy Jay?"

"Mommy likes what you're doing Daddy..." Beautiee said as she pulled him into a kiss...

"Good morning!" Starr sang as she walked into the kitchen with Chandler...

"Starr!" my father beamed as he pulled me into a hug and kissed me...

"Hi Daddy..." I said as I hugged him back...

"Hi Daddy..." Chandler laughed as he went over to hug my father...

"Hello Chandler..." my father said as he hugged him back....

"Is this Lil' Bazil?" I asked as I held my arms out to take my brother...

"This is Jay..." Beautiee answered...

"He's not named after my father?"

"He is – your father's name is Bazil J. Osgood – so your brother's name is Jay – this gives him his own identity..."

"Hi Jay..." I whispered as I held out my arms for him and he wiggled to get to me... "Do you remember me?"

"Of course he remembers you..." Beautiee laughed...

"Really?"

"Yes Starr – babies can hear at 4 months..."

"They can?" I asked as my father and Chandler turned around...

"Yes... they can..." Beautiee answered... "Chandler – have some coffee..." Beautiee said as she hugged Chandler...

"Thank you – I will..."

"Can I ask you something?" I asked...

"Yes Starr?"

"When I... caught you..."

"Yes... when you caught us..." Beautiee sighed...

"I'm sorry – never mind..."

"Go 'head Starr – ask your question..."

96

"Do the babies hear that?"

"Yes Starr – the babies hear everything – including sex..." Chandler and I looked at each other and smiled. I caught my father looking at us but he didn't say anything...

"What was it like?" I asked as my father sat at the table with more coffee for us...

"I was in labor at your reception, I went to the bathroom... and then my water broke..."

"Your water broke?"

"The baby is in a sack called the placenta. When it breaks, the liquid comes out – also known as – the water broke..."

"How do you know when that happens?"

"It feels like you peed on yourself..."

"Ooohhh..." I laughed. Chandler looked at me and smiled. I caught my father watching us again too...

"Once the water breaks... the pains come..."

"Would you do it again?"

"Yea..." Beautiee answered as she looked at my father and smiled...

"I'm happy my mother was there..." I said as Jay started fidgeting...

"Let Chandler hold him..." Beautiee said...

"Okay – here Chandler – take him..."

"He's so little..." Chandler said...

"Go ahead Chandler – you won't hurt him..." my father said...

"Hey brother-in-law Jay – I'm your sister's husband – Chandler..." he said as he smiled at Jay...

"I'm glad your mother was there too – she really helped me with my labor pain...

"I couldn't believe it when I saw Jermoll..."

"What did you say?" Beautiee asked...

"I couldn't believe it when I saw Jermoll..."

"Who's Jermoll?"

"Officer Thompson..." Chandler answered...

"Jermoll... is Officer Thompson?" Beautiee asked...

"Yes – and he was with my mother on our wedding night..." I laughed...

"Give me my son..." Beautiee said...

"Did I do something wrong?" Chandler asked...

"No Chandler – he's hungry – I need to feed him – I'ma take him in the other room...

"Can I come Beautiee?" I asked...

"Sure Starr – c'mon..." Beautiee said as she took Jay and I followed them into the living room... "Okay Jay – time to eat..." Beautiee said as she took her breast out and Jay latched on...

"Ooohhh... can I take a picture? Please?"

"Yes Starr..." Beautiee sighed. She looked so beautiful feeding my brother... and I captured it...

"I can't wait to have children with Chandler..." I sighed...

"Enjoy being married first..."

"Why?"

"Because you're newlyweds..."

"We won't be happy with a baby?"

"Starr..."

"Yes Beautiee?"

"You're going to be very happy..."

"I'm confused – why did you say I should enjoy being married first?"

"Because you should..."

"I don't understand..."

"Starr..."

"Yes Beautiee?"

"Stop trying so hard..."

"I can't help it..."

"Just enjoy your husband... like I'm enjoying your father..."

"Oohhh... I get it..."

"I loved your father from the moment I met him... and now that we have a son together..."

"What Beautiee?"

"I love him even more..." she said as Jay nodded off on Beautiee's breast...

"Oh look... he fell asleep..." I laughed...

"That's what he does – he drinks until he gets full – and then he sleeps..."

"What does it taste like?"

"You wanna taste it?"

"Beautiee... I can't..."

"Sure you can – give me your hand..."

"Okay..." Beautiee took my hand, put it under her breast, squeezed her nipple, and a few drops of milk hit my hand...

"Taste it..."

"Okay..." I said as I licked my hand... "Hmmm... it's kinda sweet..."

"Yes... it is – c'mon – I'm gonna put him to bed – then we'll go back into the kitchen with our husbands..."

"I like that – our husbands..." I sighed as I followed Beautiee upstairs to put Jay down and then we went back downstairs to join my father and Chandler in the kitchen...

"Maybe now that Mary has a man in her life she'll leave us the hell alone..." Bazil laughed...

"Maybe – I can't believe Jermoll though..."

"Why not?"

"I didn't think Jermoll would ever settle down - especially with Mary..."

"What makes you say that?"

"Rumor has it that some of the officers get involved with the prisoners... to pass the time... but they never get serious with them..."

"I see..."

"I'm happy for Jermoll – if Mary makes him happy – good for him – and good for her..." Bazil was seething... but Chandler couldn't see it...

"Tell me something Chandler..."

"What's that?"

"Did you..."

"Yes..."

"Did you ever hurt them?"

"Never..."

"Never?"

"Never..."

"What changed?"

"I wanted a wife..."

"My daughter..."

"Yes..."

"Did Jermoll ever hurt anyone?"

"Not that I know of..."

"What do you mean?"

"No one ever made a complaint against Jermoll... or any other officer..."

"Where's Jay?" my father asked as Beautiee and I walked into the kitchen...

"He's upstairs... in bed..." I answered...

"I need to get my belly full too..." my father said...

"Sound's good..." Chandler said...

"Okay – let's see what I can come up with..." my father said as he turned on the oven. I watched my father take out the turkey bacon, put it on the tray, put the biscuits on another tray, take out the eggs, cream, and three cheeses – parmesan, American, and cheddar. My father scrambled one dozen eggs combined with the three cheeses, added the cream, and beat them until they were bright yellow. My father took 4 potatoes out of the refrigerator, washed them, chopped them, and put them in a cast-iron frying pan with olive oil. The oven was ready and he put the turkey bacon and biscuits into the oven and then he put the eggs into another frying pan with olive oil and butter...

"Damn that smells good..." Chandler said. My father didn't respond – he just continued cooking as we sat at the table...

"Bazil doesn't like to be disturbed when he's cooking..." Beautiee laughed...

"I see..." Chandler laughed...

"It'll be worth it..." Beautiee said. I watched my father make the plates. I knew better than to ask if he needed help – he was so meticulous in his preparation. When he brought them to the table we were in awe...

"Damn this looks good!" Chandler said...

"It is..." Beautiee said...

"Thank you Daddy – Thank you Lord – Amen!" I said...

"Amen!" Beautiee, Chandler, and my father said in unison...

"Daddy – can you teach me to cook like this?" I asked as we ate...

"No..."

"Why not Daddy?"

"You're my daughter... cooking is in your blood..."

"It is?"

"It is..."

"How will I know?"

"Starr?"

"Yes Chandler?"

"Do you remember the first time you cooked for me?"

"Yes..." I sighed...

"You went into the kitchen, you took out food, you cooked it... and it was delicious..." Chandler said as he pulled me into a kiss...

"Thank you..."

"I fell in love with you right away..."

"Aww..." Beautiee said as my father watched us...

"See? Like is said – it's in your blood..." my father said...

"I wish my mother could be here..." I sighed. Nobody said anything...

"Have you seen your mother?" Beautiee asked...

"Not since we've been back from our honeymoon...

"Are you going to see her today?"

"I'm not sure..."

"How was your honeymoon?" my father asked...

"It was everything..." Chandler answered...

"We didn't really have a honeymoon... at that time..." my father said...

"You didn't?" Chandler asked...

"No..."

"Why not?"

"I met Beautiee that night... I asked her to marry me the next day – we went to Vegas – and got married..."

"You only knew Beautiee for 24 hours?"

"It was actually less than that..." my father said as he came up behind Beautiee and kissed her...

"Wow..."

"I couldn't let her get away..." my father said as he held her...

"And I couldn't leave you..." Beautiee said...

"Aww... that's beautiful..." Chandler said...

"I still can't believe it..." Beautiee said...

"I hope my mother will be happy with Jermoll..." I sighed...

"I'm sure she will be Starr..." Beautiee said...

"Oh my God – what if they have a baby?" I laughed....

"What's so funny?" Chandler asked...

"Then I would have two brothers – from two mothers – and they could grow up together..." I sighed...

"I'm not feeling well – I need to go lay down..." Beautiee said as she got up from the table...

"Sorry – we did get you up kinda early..." Chandler said...

"I'll be fine – I just need some sleep..." Beautiee said...

"Okay – c'mon Starr – we'll get going – it's early – let's go wake up your mother –maybe cooking's in her blood too..." Chandler laughed as we got up from the table...

"Still hungry?" my father laughed as we headed for the door...

"Not really – I just like to eat!" Chandler said as we all laughed...

"Love y'all...' Beautiee said as she pulled us all into a hug...

"Love you too..." Chandler said...

"Love you too..." my father said...

"Love you – bye Daddy – bye Beautiee..." I said as we left...

"Bazil..." Beautiee whispered as she started crying...

"I know..." Bazil said as he pulled Beautiee into a hug and held her...

"She won't let it go..."

"Who?"

"Starr..."

"What do you mean?"

"When we went shopping for the wedding..."

"I know... I'm sorry..." Bazil said as he kissed her...

"She saw us arguing... I covered for Mary..."

"I know..."

"We had a beautiful wedding... we had the baby... Mary helped me..."

"Yes... I know..."

"When I dropped Starr off she told me she knew I was mad at her mother..."

"She did..."

"I told her I was about to get mad..."

"I didn't know that..."

"She promised me she wouldn't bring it up again..."

"Okay..."

"Of all the men in the world – why Thompson?" Beautiee cried...

"I know... I know..."

"When she started talking about them having a baby and our children growing up together... she literally made me sick to my stomach..."

"I know..."

"She constantly brings up her mother... I'm trying so hard... but I can't do it Bazil..." Beautiee cried...

"I know..."

"She's so happy... and I'm happy for her... and I love her... but I can't do it..."

"What are you saying? You don't want Starr to come around anymore?"

"Bazil – I love Starr – I would never ask you to give her up... but I can't be anywhere near Jermoll – they can't have a baby – we can't be a family – he needs to die..." she cried...

"I know..."

"You do?"

"Yes..."

"Oh Bazil..."

"I had a conversation with Chandler earlier while you were feeding Jay..."

"You did?"

"Yes..."

"Did you tell him?"

"I can't tell him... it'll destroy him..."

"It'll destroy me too..."

"I know..."

"What did Chandler say?"

"Chandler said there were rumors... but no one ever filed a complaint..."

"Smalls knows..."

"I know..."

"He wanted me to file a complaint... maybe I should have..."

"I'm glad you didn't...

"Why?"

"You'd been through so much already... I just wanted you home..."

"I wanted that too..."

"I asked Chandler if he ever hurt anyone..."

"Did he?"

"Never..."

"Oh thank God..."

"You're welcome..." God said...

"I asked him what changed..."

"What did he say?"

"He said he wanted a wife..."

"I wish Thompson found somebody else – why'd it have to be Mary?" Beautiee cried...

"I know..."

"She can have children – just like I can..."

"I know..."

"What are we gonna do? I thought we were finally in a good place and we could be happy – and now here come's Starr with this bullshit – when will it fuckin' end?" Beautiee cried...

"I'm sorry..." Bazil whispered as he started crying.

Chapter 12

"Let me turn on the scanner and see what's happening..." Chandler said as he reached over to turn it on...

"Are you going into work today?"

"No Starr – we can go see your mother if you want..."

"I'd like that..."

"Okay then..." Chandler said as we headed to Downtown Bridgeport...

"Shots fired – officer down – officer down..."

"Oh my God..." I whispered...

"Starr... shhh..." Chandler said as he turned up the scanner...

"All available units – requesting assistance – Trumbull Gardens..."

"I'm glad my mother doesn't live there anymore..."

"Starr – I need to get you home – I gotta go..."

"Chandler – you said..."

"Starr! Not now!" Chandler yelled as he turned on the siren and sped down the highway...

"I'm sorry..."

"Starr – I'm sorry – but this is my life..."

"I know..."

"I'm going to get you home – then I need to go..."

"Promise me you'll come back to me Chandler..." I whispered as I started crying. Chandler got off at the next exit. He pulled into the first available parking lot and parked the car...

"Why are we stopping?"

"Come here..." Chandler said as he reached over and unbuckled my seat belt...

"Okay..." I whispered as I moved closer to Chandler and he held me...

"I'm sorry..."

"I know..."

"This is my job... this is my life... this is our life..."

"I don't want to lose you..."

"You won't lose me Starr..."

"You promise?"

"I promise..."

"I want to have your children..."

"I want that too..."

"I need you to come home..." I cried...

"I'll always come home Starr..." Chandler said as he kissed me... "But I have to leave..."

"Why?"

"Starr – I'm a Sergeant – those are my men – when they need me – I need to be there..."

"Always?"

"Always..."

"What if you get hurt?"

"I can't promise you I won't get hurt..."

"Chandler... please..."

"Starr... I need you to be strong..."

"I can't..."

"Starr... you're your father's daughter..."

"Chandler... I can't..."

"Starr – listen to me..." Chandler said as he took my face in his hands... "I know this is a lot for you – but I need you to focus..."

"You sound like my mother..."

"Good..."

"No it's not..."

"Starr – I need you to be my wife..." he said as he kissed me... "And I need you to understand everything that comes with that..."

"Okay..."

"Can you do this?"

"Yes Chandler..."

"I don't know what'll happen when I get there..."

"I know...

"I'm going to need you to be strong – especially when I'm weak..."

"Chandler – you're never weak..."

"I have my moments – you'll see them..."

"No I won't..."

"Starr – listen to me..."

"Okay..."

"There will be days when I come home... and I'll need you to comfort me..."

"I will Chandler..."

"And I'll need you to be strong for me..."

"I will Chandler..."

"I can get through anything – as long as I have you..."

"You will Chandler..."

"Some wives leave..."

"I won't leave...

"Promise me..."

"I promise..."

"Say it..." Chandler said as he kissed me...

"I promise... I'll never leave you Chandler..."

"And I promise..." he said as he kissed me again... "I'll always come home to you... but now... I need to get you home... and I need to go..." Chandler said as he started the car and we rode the rest of the way without speaking until we got to Bridgeport...

"I'll wait up..." I said as I went to open the door...

"Starr... wait..." Chandler said as he unbuckled his seat belt, got out, and came around to open door for me. When I got out, he took me in his arms and held me... "I love you..."

"I love you too..."

"I have to go..."

"I know..." Chandler kissed me hard and I held on tight until he let me go, got back in the car, and drove off...

"Good afternoon Mrs. Chandler..." the doorman said when he saw me...

"Good afternoon..." I said as I got in the elevator...

"Hey Starr – you're back!" Theresa said as I walked up to my door...

"Yes... I'm back..."

"How was your honeymoon?"

"Wonderful..." I answered as I opened my door, went inside and closed it. I went into the kitchen, turned on the scanner, and listened so I'd know what was happening...

"Officer in critical condition – Bridgeport Hospital..."

"Hi Mommy..." I sighed as I answered the phone..."

"What's wrong?"

"It's Chandler..."

"Is he okay?"

"No..."

"Is he hurt?"

"He's at the hospital..."

"Oh my God – what happened? Why aren't you with him?"

"Chandler needs me to be here..."

"I don't understand..."

"One of his officers is in critical condition – he had to go..."

"Oh Starr... I'm sorry..."

"I just want him to come home!" I cried...

"He will Starr..."

"I can't lose him Mommy!"

"You won't Starr..."

"Thompson DOA..."

"What's that Starr?" my mother asked...
"It's a scanner Mommy..."
"What did they just say?"
"I wasn't listening..." I lied...
"Starr?"
"Yes Mommy?"
"What did they just say?"
"I need to go now..." I said as I hung up...
"Chandler..." I whispered as I answered the phone...
"He's gone..."
"I know..."
"You know?"
"I was listening..."
"You turned on the scanner..."
"Yes..."
"Why?"
"I needed to be with you Chandler..."
"I need to be with you too..."
"My mother knows..."
"She does?"
"She heard..."
"I need to go now..."
"I love you..."
"I love you too..." Chandler said before he hung up. I turned off the scanner and waited for Chandler. A few hours later I heard him put his key in the door. I went over to him, put is head on my shoulder, stood there, and let him cry.

Chapter 13

"We interrupt your regularly scheduled programming to bring you the following..." Bazil listened as he tuned up News 12...

"Earlier today, there was a shooting at Trumbull Gardens. Officers arrived on the scene to assist – several people were injured and several arrests were made; however, we are sorry to report that Officer Jermoll Thompson was pronounced dead upon arrival at Bridgeport Hospital. Another officer remains in critical condition at Bridgeport Hospital. Stay tuned to News 12 for updates..."

"Oh my God..." Bazil whispered...

"What's wrong?" Beautiee yawned...

"Thompson's dead..."

"What?" Beautiee asked as she sat up in bed...

"There was a shooting at Trumbull Gardens... some of the officers were injured... one's in critical condition at Bridgeport Hospital... Thompson was pronounced dead when he arrived..."

"Wow..." Beautiee smiled to herself. Bazil caught her smiling but he didn't say anything... "I wonder how Chandler's doing?"

"Not well..."

"Probably not..."

"I'll call Starr and check on him..."

"Okay..." Beautiee yawned as she got up out of bed to go get Jay...

"Hi Daddy..."

"How's Chandler..?"

"He's not good..."

"How are you?"

"I'm not good either..."

"I'm sorry Starr..."

"I know Daddy..."

"He'll be in the news, in front of cameras..."

"Oh my God... does he have to?"

"Yes Starr..."

"Do I have to?"

"No Starr – Chandler won't want you anywhere that..."

"I don't know what to do Daddy..."

"You know exactly what to do... you're my daughter..."

"All I know is I love him..."

"Exactly..." Bazil said as he hung up...

"How's she doing?" Beautiee asked as she fed Jay...

"She's not good..."

"She'll be alright..."

"I wish I knew that..."

116

"You didn't think I'd be alright either and here I am..."

"You're right..." Bazil said as he stood up, went over to Beautiee and held her as she fed Jay...

"Starr can't be Daddy's lil' girl forever — she has to grow up..."

"I know... but..."

"You can't coddle her Bazil — you have to let her go through this — it will make her a better wife — a stronger wife — for Chandler..."

"Beautiee..."

"I went through worse — and I made it — and we have a son — and after everything we've been through — after everything you put me through — I love your more..."

"Beautiee..." Bazil whispered as he started crying...

"I love you more..." Beautiee said again as she kissed him...

"I love you so much..."

"I love you more..."

"Mommy loves me more..." Bazil said as he took Jay from Beautiee and held him...

"And Starr will love Chandler more..."

"Starr will love him more..." Bazil said as he pulled Beautiee to him, held her, and kissed her.

"Starr..." my mother whispered as she answered the phone...

"Hi Mommy..."

"Starr... I can't believe it..." she cried...

"I'm sorry Mommy..."

"It's not your fault..."

"I can come over..."

"No Starr... stay with Chandler..."

"Mommy... you shouldn't be alone..."

"Starr... you just got back from your honeymoon... you should be with your husband..."

"Mommy... Chandler will understand..."

"Starr... no..."

"I'm coming to see you..."

"You can stop by tomorrow after work..."

"Okay..."

"How was your honeymoon?"

"It was wonderful..."

"How's Lil' Bazil?"

"Beautiee says his name is Jay..."

"What does your father say?"

"Daddy calls him Jay too..."

"If he were my son – he'd be Bazil – just like his father..."

"Mommy?"

"Yes Starr?"

"How'd I get my name?"

"You're my Starr..."

"Aww..."

"Did you ever want a son?"

"I wanted whatever God chose for me to have..."

"I can't wait to have Chandler's children..."

"That'll be nice..."

"I want a boy... and a girl..."

"Chandler should have a son..."

"Yes he should..."

"I'll be a grandmother..."

"Yes you will..."

"That'll make me happy..."

"I'll get right on it Mommy..."

"Starr – don't have children for me..."

"I'm not Mommy..." I laughed...

"He asked me to marry him..."

"Who?"

"Jermoll..."

"I'm sorry Mommy..."

"So am I..."

"Did you say yes?"

"Yes... I did..."

"Aww..."

"I was engaged for a brief moment... and now it's gone..."

"I'm sorry Mommy..."

"I'm not..."

"You're not?"

"No..."

"Why?"

"Because I know he loved me..."

"Aww..."

"That'll get me through this..."

"Hold on Mommy – Chandler's on the news..." I said as I turned up the television...

"We interrupt your regularly scheduled programming to bring you this update: earlier yesterday afternoon, there was a shooting in

Trumbull Gardens. Several officers were injured, and several arrests were made; however, unfortunately Officer Jermoll Thompson was pronounced dead at Bridgeport Hospital. The other officer was reported in critical condition; however, his condition is now being reported as stable. Sergeant Corbett was on the scene and at the hospital, but declined to comment. We now return to our regularly scheduled programming…"

"Mommy?" Are you still there?" My mother didn't answer me. She had put the phone down and I could hear her crying in the background… so I hung up.

"Good morning Amy…" I answered…

"Good morning Starr…" Amy said… "Listen – normally I wouldn't call you on Sunday but I had to call you and give Chandler my condolences…"

"Thank you Amy – that's very sweet…"

"How's Chandler?"

"He's… Chandler… I'm sorry… I don't really know what to say…"

"That's okay Starr – it's perfectly understandable – I remember the first time I went through it with my son…"

"You went through this too?"

"Honey – my son's a Sergeant too – of course I've been through it…"

"How do you deal with it?"

120

"You just do – Chandler's lucky to have you..."

"I don't really know what to do for him..."

"Just be his wife – that's all he needs..."

"That's what my father said..."

"You're father's an amazing man..."

"Thank you..."

"Does he get along with Chandler?"

"Yes... Chandler calls him Daddy sometimes..." I laughed...

"Aww... that's funny..." Amy laughed...

"Will your son be there tomorrow?"

"We'll all be there tomorrow..."

"You will?"

"Yes Starr... and so will you..."

"I'll be there?"

"Yes Starr... the wives go too..."

"Do I say anything?"

"Starr – just be yourself – you'll be fine..."

"Okay..."

"We'll see you tomorrow..."

"Okay Amy... bye..."

"Who was that?" Chandler yawned...

"Amy... she called to give her condolences and to give me advice..."

"You don't need any advice Starr..."

"I don't really know what I'm supposed to do Chandler..."

"Starr... come here..."

"Okay..." I said as I went over to Chandler and he pulled me into a hug...

"Do you love me?"

"Yes Chandler..."

"See..." he said as he kissed me... "You know exactly what to do..."

"What about tomorrow?"

"What about tomorrow?"

"What do I do?"

"Just be yourself..."

"That's what Amy said..."

"I'm glad she called you..."

"Me too..."

"Now..." Chandler said as he kissed me again... "We have business we need to attend to..."

"We do?"

"Yes... Mrs. Corbett..." he said as he kissed my neck and shoulders...

"Where do we start... Mr. Corbett?" I asked as Chandler turned me around and kissed me fully...

"Right... here..." Chandler said as he picked me up, wrapped my legs around him, and laid me down on our bed.

Chapter 14

"Good morning Mrs. Osgood..." Bazil said as he kissed Beautiee awake...

"Good morning... Mr. Osgood..." Beautiee breathed...

"What would you like..." he asked as he kissed her... "to do... today?"

"You..."

"Me?"

"Yes... you..." Beautiee said as she pulled Bazil down on top of her...

"I'd love to... do... you... too..." Bazil breathed as he spread her legs and put his tongue in her mouth... "Mmmph... Mmmph..."

"My breasts are full..."

"Mmmm... I know..." Bazil breathed as he started sucking her left breast..."

"Bazil... stop..."

"Why?" Bazil asked as he continued sucking...

"Jay... he'll be hungry..."

"So..."

"So... I want to feed him..."

"Okay... I'll leave him some milk..." Bazil laughed...

123

"Hurry up..."

"Say please..."

"Please..."

"Please what?"

"Please fuck me..."

"Okay..." Bazil breathed as he eased himself inside her...

"Oh... Bazil... fuck..."

"Is this what you want?"

"Yes Bazil... yes..."

"Uuummmpphhh.... Yes..." Bazil breathed in Beautiee's ear as he picked up the pace...

"Huhhh... Huhhh... Huhhh..."

"Ummph... Ummph... Ummph..."

"Huhhh... Huhhh... Huhhh..."

"Ummph... Ummph... Ummph..." Jay started crying just as Beautiee was about to cum..."

"Jay's awake..." Bazil breathed...

"I know..."

"He's hungry...

"Oh... yes..."

"He needs to eat..."

"Yes... yes... yes... Huhh... Huuhh..."

Ummph... Ummph... Ummph... Ummph..."

"Waaaaah!" Jay started crying a little louder...

"Daddy's... coming... Jay... Uuuugggghhhh!" Bazil collapsed on top of Beautiee and lay there inside her as Jay cried...

"Jay... Daddy's coming... give him a minute..." Beautiee laughed...

"He's hungry..." Bazil said as he kissed her...

"He's not starving – he's just spoiled..." Beautiee said as she wrapped her legs around him so he couldn't get up...

"Beautiee... let me get him..."

"I will..." she said as she kissed him...

"He doesn't like to wait..."

"Neither do I..." she said as she kissed him again...

"I'll be right back..." he said as he kissed her... "I promise..."

"I know..." Beautiee said as she unlocked her legs and let Bazil get up. Bazil went to get Jay and came back...

"Come here Jay..." Beautiee said as she took him in her arms... "When you wake up – I need you to wait a few minutes before you get antsy..." she said as she put her breast in his mouth... "We won't keep you waiting long... I promise..."

"Okay Mommy..." Jay cooed. When he had his fill, Beautiee put him down beside her...

"Let's go introduce Jay to the office..."

"Okay..." Bazil smiled...

"C'mon Jay – I need to put you back in your room so we can get dressed..." Beautiee said as she started to leave with him and he started fussing...

"Let him stay..." Bazil said...

"Okay... you can stay Jay... but I don't want any fussing..." Beautiee said as she got up and went towards the shower...

"What are you doing?" Bazil asked...

"I'm taking a shower..."

"With Jay?"

"Are you coming Daddy?" Beautiee asked as she dropped her robe and walked into the shower with Jay...

"Daddy's coming Jay..." Bazil laughed as he joined them.

When they got to the office, Sam was the first one to see them...

"Oh my God! Hi!" Sam beamed as hugged them all...

"Hello Sam..." Bazil said...

"Hello Sam..." Beautiee said... "This is Jay..."

"Hi Jay..." Sam said as Joselyn came around the corner...

"Oh my God – le'me see – move Sam!" she laughed as she took Jay out of Beautiee's arms...

"Umm... could you give me back my son? Please?" Beautiee laughed...

"Mrs. Osgood – I"m sorry – here..." she said as she went to give Jay back...

"It's okay – you can hold him..." Beautiee laughed...

"Isn't he cute Sam?" Joselyn beamed...

"Yea..." Sam laughed...

"Oh my goodness – you brought the baby – heeyyyy!" Sheila said as she came over to see Jay... "Oh he's cute – what's his name?"

"His name's Jay..." Sam answered...

"Oh lord – another Jay..." Sheila laughed as she took him from Joselyn... "That's okay – you can be Jay – at least you're cute..."

"Oh lord – Mommy – don't start..." Joselyn laughed...

"I'm surprised you're here already – we didn't even know you had the baby – I thought you weren't due for another month..." Sheila said...

"I wasn't..."

"Oh Wow – how was the labor?" Joselyn asked...

"C'mon – let's go to the cafeteria – I need coffee..." Beautiee said as they all went to the cafeteria and sat down...

"I'll get coffee... y'all stay here – I'll be right back – c'mon Sam..." Joselyn said...

"So much for her getting coffee..." Sam laughed as he went to get coffee with Joselyn...

"He's a happy baby – he's not even trying to get away from me..." Sheila said...

"He's a very happy baby..." Bazil said...

"Okay – I'm back..." Joselyn said as she sat down with coffee for all of us...

"Mmmm... ˙ damn Joselyn – I'ma need to give you another raise – you make coffee better than anybody I know..." Beautiee laughed...

"Okay!" Joselyn laughed...

"Does she make coffee better than me?" Bazil asked...

"Yes Bazil... sorry..." Beautiee answered...

"That's fine... remember that..." Bazil laughed...

"So... about my labor..." Beautiee said as they drank coffee...

"What happened?" Sheila asked...

"I knew Jay was coming early – I felt it..."

"How..." Joselyn asked...

"You just know Joselyn – you'll understand when you get pregnant – go 'head Beautiee..." Sheila said...

"So my water broke while I was at the reception!!"

"No!"

"Yes... I had the baby at the Bed and Breakfast..."

"You had the baby on their wedding night?"

"Yes..."

"Was it a long labor?" Joselyn asked...

"It wasn't long – but it hurt like hell..." Beautiee laughed...

"I'm sorry..." Bazil said as he pulled Beautiee into a kiss...

"You need to be sorry – we go through a lot to bring you men into this world..." Sheila said...

"Oh boy – why'd you have to get my mother started!" Joselyn laughed...

"Every time somebody has a baby she relives her own labor!" Sam laughed...

"Was it that bad Mommy?" Joselyn asked...

"Yes – all 23 hours of it – all natural – yes – it was that bad!"

"I'm so sorry Mommy..." Joselyn said...

"That's okay Joselyn – it wasn't your fault – it was your father's fault..."

"So why don't you tell him then? Why you always tellin' me?" Joselyn laughed...

"'Cause he don't work here – and you can't tell me shut up!" Sheila laughed...

"Bazil was shook – he didn't know what to do – he held my hand and kept kissing me and telling me he loved me every time a labor pain hit..." Beautiee laughed...

"Aww shoot... le'me find out... see Joselyn – that's what your father should'a did..."

"Oh lord – please – I can't take it..." Joselyn laughed...

"Mary helped me by rubbing my back when the pains hit too..."

"Mary? Mary that used to work here?" Joselyn asked...

"Yea..."

"How... never mind..."

"Well I wanna know!" Sheila laughed...

"Everyone was asleep – we woke them up..."

"Oh my God – you were that loud?" Joselyn asked...

"Girl – when them pains hit – you don't give a damn who hears your mouth!" Sheila said...

"So Starr, Chandler, and Mary were in the room with us... and I delivered the baby – and Starr recorded it..."

"No! It was their wedding night! He wasn't supposed to be between your legs!" Sheila laughed...

"He wasn't – Starr was..." Beautiee laughed...

"Bazil! Why weren't you between her legs?" Sheila snapped...

"I was... when she started pushing..." Bazil answered...

"And did you cut the cord?"

"Yes Maam..."

"Okay... that's better..."

"Sam – I'ma need you to take notes – my Momma's crazy..." Joselyn laughed...

"Doesn't matter – it didn't stop me from marrying you did it?" Sam asked...

"Sure didn't!" Joselyn laughed...

"I know that's right Sam!" Beautiee laughed as they high-fived..."

"We gotta get going – let's stop by the office so I can feed him right quick before we leave..." Beautiee said as she stood up..."

"He's fine – you don't need to feed him..." Sheila laughed...

"Joselyn..."

"Don't even say it Beautiee!" Joselyn laughed...

"Here's your son – hopefully I'll be holding my grandchild one day..." Sheila said as she looked at Joselyn...

"We can leave with them – and start working on your grandchild today – if you want..." Sam laughed...

"You can work on my grandchild on your own time – this is company time – I need those stats..." Sheila said...

"Uh huh – see Joselyn – that's how you get her to stop all that..." Sam laughed...

"C'mon y'all..." Joselyn laughed as we headed to the office...

"It was great seeing y'all – come back soon – and bring baby Jay – he'll keep my mother occupied..." Joselyn laughed...

"I still want my grandchild!" Sheila snapped...

"Le'me hurry up and get you those stats..." Sam laughed as Joselyn, Sheila, and Sam left the office...

"Jay – you want something else to eat?" Beautiee asked as she pulled out her breast. Jay sucked on it a little and then stopped... "Hmm... not hungry now – okay – I'll put it back..." Beautiee said as she went to put her breast away...

"Beautiee... wait a minute..." Bazil said as he went over to her and put her breast in his mouth...

131

"Bazil... stop it..." Beautiee laughed...

"Jay's not hungry... that means more for me..."

"Bazil – we can't – not with the baby..."

"Doesn't stop you at home..."

"Yes – at home – but we're not home now..." she laughed...

"See Jay... Daddy's nasty..." Bazil laughed...

"Bazil! Don't tell him that!" Beautiee laughed as she pulled her breast out Bazil's mouth and put it back in her bra...

"Mommy... I already know Daddy's nasty... and you're nasty too..." Jay laughed...

"Whatchu laughin' at Jay?" Bazil asked...

"He's laughin' at your ass!" Beautiee laughed...

"Where would you like to go for breakfast?" Bazil asked...

"Let's go see Dr. Julianne!" Beautiee squealed...

"Really? For Breakfast?" Bazil laughed...

"I want her to see the baby..."

"I want her to see the baby too..."

"We can eat there..." Beautiee said as they drove off...

"I love you..." Bazil said as he took her hand and kissed it...

"I love you too." They drove the rest of the way listening to Jay coo and laugh to himself. When they got to Portchester Beautiee called Dr. Julianne's office...

"Dr. Julianne's office – this is Dawn…"

"Hi Dawn – it's Beautiee…"

"Hi Beautiee – how are you?"

"We're downstairs – can we come up?"

"Ohhh – shoot – we're over-booked…"

"That's okay – I just wanna say hello…"

"Okay – c'mon up…" Dawn said as she hung up…

"Dawn – I need you to get me ready for our next patient…" Dr. Julianne said…

"Beautiee's on her way up…"

"Oh my – I can't possibly see her today!"

"She just wants to say hello…"

"Okay – I'll say hello – then we need to get back to those patients…"

"Hi everybody!" Beautiee said as she came in with Bazil and Jay…

"Oh wow! Can I see?" one of the patients asked…

"Sure…" Beautiee said as she let the patient hold Jay…

"Oh he's cute!"

"Thank you - his name is Jay…" Bazil said…

"Hi Jay!" the lady said…

"Who's baby is that?" Dr. Julianne asked as she came over…

"This is our baby!" Beautiee beamed…

"Oh my goodness – you weren't due for another month – congratulations! Can I hold him?"

"Yes you can…" Bazil said…

"Dawn look – Beautiee had the baby – I guess I was wrong – he's a beautiful boy..."

"Thank you Dr. Julianne..."

"Thank you for stopping by – have you had your check up yet?"

"No..."

"You'll need to come see me soon – and bring him with you..."

"I will Dr. Julianne..."

"Where was he born?" Dawn asked...

"He was born June 6th at the Taylor Bed and Breakfast in Boston..."

"Oh wow – a 2nd honeymoon?" Dawn asked...

"Our daughter's wedding..."

"Your daughter's wedding? The one you told me about?" Dr. Julianne asked...

"Yes Dr. Julianne..." Bazil answered...

"Oh my God – that's wonderful – congratulations!" Dr. Julianne said...

"Thank you Dr. Julianne..." Mary said as she came into the waiting room...

"Oh hi Mary – I was just talking to Beautiee..."

"Yes I know – it was my daughter that got married..."

"Oh... I see..."

"Hi Mary..." Beautiee said...

"Hi Beautiee – is Dr. Julianne your doctor too?"

"Yes she is..."

"Oh wow – small world..." Mary laughed... "I guess you're gonna need a new doctor now huh?" Mary laughed...

"No – I'm staying with Dr. Julianne..."

"How can you stay with her? She doesn't deliver babies..."

"I don't need her to deliver our baby – he's already here remember?" I laughed...

"Oh shoot – le'me see Lil' Bazil..."

"His name is Jay..." Bazil corrected...

"Jay? Huh – if he was my son he'da been named after you..."

"He's not your son – he's my son – and his name is Jay..." Beautiee said as she walked over to Bazil and stood beside him holding Jay..."

"Can I see him?"

"He's right here..." Beautiee said...

"Le'me hold him..." Mary said as she came over towards Beautiee with her arms out to take him...

"No... I need to feed him – c'mon Bazil – let's go – bye everybody!" Beautiee yelled...

"Bye Beautiee – by Mr. Osgood – thanks for stopping by – congratulations!" Dr. Julianne said as she went back to see another patient...

"Beautiee – I'll schedule you for 5 weeks from today..." Dawn said as they walked out the door and got in the elevator...

"Fuckin' Bitch!" Beautiee snapped...

"Beautiee... clam down..." Bazil said...

"Don't tell me to calm the fuck down – you heard what she said – what the fuck is she doing

135

here anyway – Dr. Julianne doesn't even take Medicaid – I wish...Mmmm...." Beautiee moaned as Bazil took her in his arms, held her, and kissed her deeply...

"Now..." Bazil said between kisses... "I need... you... to go... back... to that... happy... place..."

"Which one?" Beautiee asked as they stopped on another floor and another couple got on the elevator...

"The place... where... everyone... was happy... to see... Jay..."

"Aww... honey look – they have a newborn..." the lady said...

"Reminds me of us..." her husband said as he kissed his wife...

"Aww... I want us to be like that when we get older..." Beautiee said...

"The way you two are all over each other – that shouldn't be a problem..." his wife laughed...

"Sorry about that – my husband can't stand to see me upset – he'll do anything to calm me down..." Beautiee said...

"Smart man..." her husband laughed...

"Is he your first?" the wife asked...

"No... we have a 22 year old daughter..." Beautiee answered...

"Oh my goodness! How old are you?"

"I'm 30 – he's 40..."

"Blended family..." her husband said...

"Yes..." Bazil said...

"Blended families have their challenges... but they also have their rewards..." the husband said as they got off the elevator..."

"We're going to the cafeteria – why don't you join us?" Beautiee asked...

"We'd love too – thank you for asking..." his wife said...

"You're welcome – it's so nice to meet people who understand..." Beautiee laughed...

"Oh we understand – believe me..." his wife laughed...

"I'm Beautiee – this is my husband Bazil – and this is our son Jay..."

"Bazil Osgood?" the husband asked...

"Yes sir..."

"Honey – wait 'till I tell the guys!" he beamed...

"The guys?" Bazil laughed...

"I'm Christine – this is James..." Christine said as she hugged Beautiee and Jay...

"Nice to meet you Christine... Nice to meet you James..." Beautiee said...

"Call me Chrissy..."

"Okay... Chrissy..."

"My wife has a book club that meets at our house once a month – they've read some of your books – you're Osgood Publishing right?" James asked as they sat down at a table...

"Yes... I am..." Bazil answered...

"I can't believe we're having brunch with the Osgoods..." Chrissy said...

137

"I have a publishing company under my husband as well..." Beautiee said...

"Ohhh... under your husband... sexy..." Chrissy laughed...

"We're gonna get along just fine..." I laughed...

"What kind of books do you publish?" Chrissy asked...

"I write erotic fiction – and I publish them myself..."

Oh boy – that's right up their alley..." James laughed...

"What's the title of your latest book?" Chrissy asked...

"How Far Are You Willing To Go? Murder Is Just The Beginning..."

"Oh my God! We were just talking about your books!" Chrissy beamed...

"You were?"

"Yes! We wanted to get them for our next meeting..." Chrissy answered...

"Take down my number – 203-508-2798 – text me your information – how many members you have – and I'll give you free copies for your review and discussion..."

"Thank you!" Chrissy exclaimed as she hugged Beautiee a little too tight... and Jay squirmed... "Oh goodness – sorry Jay..." Chrissy laughed...

"Can I ask you something?" James asked...

"Sure..." Bazil answered...

"This is your first-born son – right?"

"Yes..."

"You didn't want him named after you?"

"He is named after me – my name is Bazil J. Osgood – we call him Jay so he has his own identity..."

"See? That's a great idea!" James said...

"His ex doesn't seem to think so..." Beautiee said...

"Is Jay your son? Or hers?"

"He's my son..." Beautiee answered...

"Exactly..." Chrissy said...

"Brunch is on us – I'll be right back..." James said as he went to order...

"Can I hold him?" Chrissy asked...

"Can she hold you Jay?" Beautiee asked. Jay looked over at Chrissy and smiled...

"I'll take that as the cutest lil' yes I've gotten in a long, long, time!" Chrissy beamed as she took Jay and held him...

"Here's brunch!" James said as he sat down with plates...

"Oh my God – this looks delicious!" Beautiee said...

"It does..." Bazil agreed...

"They make good food here..." Chrissy said as we started eating...

"They do – we've eaten here before..." Beautiee agreed...

"Hello Mary..." Chrissy said as Mary walked in... "This is..."

"We know each other..." Beautiee said...

"Oh wow – can I hold Lil' Bazil?" Mary asked...

"Mary – I already told you – his name is Jay..." Bazil said...

"No –you cannot hold my son..." Beautiee said as she took Jay from Chrissy...

"I'll get something to eat – then I'll join you..." Mary said as she went to get food...

"Beautiee – do you want her to join us?" Chrissy asked...

"Not really..." Beautiee sighed...

"Let her sit Beautiee..." Bazil said...

"Hi Chrissy – hi James – what brings you here?" Mary asked as she sat down at the table...

"Beautiee invited us to join her and her husband for brunch – we were just getting to know them..." Chrissy answered...

"Oh that's nice – I see you've met Lil' Bazil..."

"Mary – I specifically heard Mr. Osgood tell you that his son's name is Jay – why do you keep doing that?" Chrissy asked...

"Did I just call him Lil' Bazil? I meant Jay – I'm sorry..." Mary lied...

"I'll need to feed Jay soon..." Beautiee said...

"Let me hold him so you can finish eating..." Bazil said...

"Is he a good baby?" James asked...

"He is..." Bazil answered...

"You're daughter sure wasn't!" Mary snapped...

"I'm finished..." Beautiee said... "I'll take Jay..."

"He's okay Beautiee – sit for a minute..." Bazil said...

"Okay..." Beautiee sighed...

"So Mary – what brings you here?" Chrissy asked...

"Dr. Julianne..."

"How is she?"

"She's fine – we were just upstairs visiting..." Beautiee answered...

"Did she deliver Jay?" Chrissy asked...

"No – but she gave us our first picture of Jay..." Beautiee smiled as she looked at Bazil...

"She sure did..." Bazil said...

"Aww... you two are genuine love birds..." James said...

"Hopefully your daughter will wind up just like you..." Mary said...

"I'm sure she will Mary..." Beautiee said...

"That's nice of you to say Beautiee..." Mary said...

"Chandler really loves Starr – she's going to be very happy..." Bazil said...

"Starr? Isn't that your daughter Mary?"

"Yes – Starr is my daughter..."

"Do you know my daughter?" Bazil asked...

"No – but Mary talks about her all the time at the book club meetings..." Chrissy said...

"I see..." Bazil said...

"He's starting to squirm – are you hungry Jay?" Beautiee asked as she took him from Bazil...

"Oh my goodness – you are Bazil Jr. to a T..." Mary said...

"It was lovely meeting you both – we need to go..." Beautiee said as she got up from the table...

"It was lovely meeting both of you too..." Chrissy said...

"Nice meeting you James..." Bazil said as he shook James hand...

"Same here..." James said as he shook Bazil's hand...

"We should get together soon..." Chrissy said...

"I'd like that – call me..."

"I will – see you soon..." Chrissy said...

"See you soon..." Beautiee said as she walked out of the cafeteria and Bazil followed. Mary was seething because they left her sitting there and ignored her. When they got in the car, Beautiee took out her breast and began feeding Jay... "Bazil?"

"Yes Beautiee?"

"She's gonna make me kill her..."

Chapter 15

"Who is it?" Beautiee asked...

"It's Keisha..."

"C'mon in girl..." Beautiee said as she hugged Keisha...

"Hey Bazil, hey Starr..." Keisha said as she sat down with us...

"Hello Keisha..." my father said...

"Hi Keisha..." I said...

"Listen – since you couldn't wait 9 months to have the baby – we'll just throw you a baby shower after the fact..."

"Oh that's nice – thank you Keisha..."

"Oh good – I'll invite my mother..." I said...

"No the fuck you will not!" Beautiee snapped...

"Excuse me?" I snapped back. My father and Keisha looked back and forth between us...

"Starr – I love you to death – but you're really getting on my fuckin' nerves!"

"Beautiee..." my father tried to interrupt...

"Bazil – I told you – I'm not doing this shit anymore – I'm fuckin' tired..." Beautiee said as she started shaking and crying...

"What – what's going on?" Keisha asked...

"I'll tell you what the fucks going on – remember the co-op?"

"Beautiee – what are you talkin' about?" I asked...

"Stop playin' fuckin' dumb Starr!" Beautiee snapped...

"Beautiee... clam down... you're upsetting Jay..." my father said as he put his hand on her shoulder...

"Anyway – Keisha – you know I did that for Starr – right?"

"Yea..."

"And remember when she called Starr a Lil' Bitch?"

"Hell yea – I remember that shit!" Keisha snapped...

"Exactly – who she come cryin' to – me!" Beautiee snapped...

"I know – you right..." Keisha said as she rubbed Beautiee's arm...

"Remember when we went shopping for the wedding – right?"

"Girl – I told you – you good..."

"Exactly – so when I drop Starr off – she gon' say – I know you mad at my mother..."

"Hell yea you mad – hell – I'm mad!" Keisha snapped...

"I told you I was about to be mad at you that night – didn't I Starr?"

"Yes – I said I wouldn't bring it up again – I'm sorry!"

"So now – she gon' see her mother the other day and she asked how the baby was doing..."

"Okay – what's wrong with that?" Keisha asked...

"Starr tells her mother the baby's name is Jay – and the Bitch gon' tell her – oh if he was my son his name would be Lil' Bazil – mind you – we saw her earlier today and just had this same fuckin' conversation!"

"Oh hell no!" Keisha snapped...

"This is what the fuck I'm talkin' about – now Starr sittin' here talkin' about she gonna invite her to my house – no the fuck you're not!" Beautiee snapped...

"You're not the only baby mother my father has!" I snapped...

"See – that's where you fucked up – I'm not just his baby's mother – I'm his wife!" Beautiee said as she walked up towards me...

"Beautiee... sit down..." my father said as he came up behind her and held her...

"Fine – if my mother's not invited – I'm not either!" I snapped as I got up to leave... "And this is my father's house – not yours..." I reminded her - I regretted it as soon as I said it – but it was too late...

"Keisha – please take Jay for a moment..." Beautiee said as she got up, walked past me, and opened the front door...

"Beautiee..." my father said as he tried to get her attention... "What are you doing?"

"I'm putting YOUR DAUGHTER OUT OF YOUR HOUSE!" Beautiee answered as I got up to leave...

"Starr – sit down – Beautiee – come back here... please..." my father asked. Beautiee came back into the living room and sat down beside Keisha and then my father spoke... "Starr – you're my daughter..."

"I know..."

"I love you with all my heart..."

"I love you too Daddy..."

"You owe my wife an apology..."

"But Daddy..."

"Starr – don't make me repeat myself..."

"I'm sorry Beautiee..."

"This woman is my wife..." my father said as he put his arm around her and kissed her... "She loves me – and ˉ more importantly ˉ she loves you – and as far as this house – this isn't my house – it's her house..."

"But Daddy..."

"Everything I have is hers – and when you said what you said just now – you didn't just hurt her – you hurt me..."

"I'm sorry Daddy..." I said as I started crying...

"Save it..." my father said as he stood up... "You can go now..."

"You want me to leave?"

"Yes Starr..."

"Okay Daddy... I'm sorry..." I said as I left...

146

"Keisha?"

"Yes?"

"If you're still interested in planning a baby shower for us – I'd be happy to help..."

"That's okay Bazil – I got it – I'ma do the invites - the food - all that – give me your list..."

"You already have it..."

"Okay – Sheila, Joselyn, Sam, Smalls, Me, Troy, Starr, Chandler?"

"Yea – and ask Chandler to invite his neighbors – he likes them – Beautiee – what's their names?"

"Charles and Theresa..."

"Yea – Charles and Theresa..."

"Bazil?"

"Yes Beautiee?"

"Can we invite Sheddi?"

"Sure..."

"Okay – I'ma go – I'll see y'all later – bye Jay..." Keisha said as she gave Jay back to Beautiee...

"I'm sorry..." Beautiee whispered as she cried...

"Please don't cry..." Bazil said as he kissed her eyes and her tears...

"She hurt my feelings..."

"I know..."

"I really love her – you know that – right?"

"Yes Beautiee... I know you love her..."

"Why isn't that enough Bazil?"

"I'll talk to her again..."

"No..."

"You don't want me to talk to her?"

"Bazil... I'm all talked out..."

"What are you saying?"

"I'm saying..." she said as she kissed him... "I love you..."

"I love you too..."

"I know... you make me feel loved... you always have... even when I'm mad at you..."

"You love me more..."

"That's right... I love you more..."

"What about Starr?"

"What about her?"

"You don't want me to talk to her?"

"No... I want you to talk to me... and Jay..."

"I can do that..." Bazil said as he smiled...

"Good..." Beautiee said as she kissed him...

"Troy – you ain't gonna believe this shit!" Keisha said as she slammed the door...

"Aww... Damn! What the fuck Bazil do now? I gotta cut him off?"

"Hell no – I love that mutha fucka!" Keisha laughed...

"Oh shit!" Troy said as he ran to sit with Keisha...

"Yes! So – I go over there to tell them we're planning a baby shower..."

"Okay..." Troy smiled...

"And Starr is there..."

"Okay..."

"So she gon' say oh good – I'll invite my mother – and Beautiee said no the fuck you not!"

"What?"

"All of a sudden – she starts cryin' and shakin'…"

"She alright?"

"That's what I'm sayin' – so I ask her what's goin' on – last I heard she loves Starr like her own daughter…"

"What happened Keisha!" Troy snapped…

"Give me a minute – damn!" Troy stood there looking at his watch and tapping his foot… "See – now I'm not telling you…"

"Keisha!"

"I'm just playin' – so Beautiee tells me – I'ma shorten it – you know Beautiee got Bazil to buy a co-op for Starr so her mother wouldn't have to go to the shelter right?"

"Actually I didn't – but get to the part where you love that mutha fucka!" Troy laughed…

"Okay – so Starr got into it with her mother and her mother called her a Lil' Bitch – and Beautiee told her she didn't mean that shit – but you know she did right?"

"Hell yea she meant that shit – go 'head…"

"So – they went shopping for the wedding – Beautiee paid for everything – even after that Bitch filed a lawsuit against Bazil for $150,000 – she still took the Bitch shopping – I told her you good…"

"Damn – Bazil ain't tell me about that – how you know 'bout that?"

"Beautiee told me – anyway – after she drops Starr off – she goin' tell Beautiee – I know you mad at my mother!"

"See – that's that bullshit – I'm mad too!"

"That's what the fuck I said – so now they see her the other day..."

"Who?"

"Mary..."

"Okay..."

"She wanna see the baby so Beautiee told her the baby's name is Jay – Bitch gonna say if it was her son his name would be Lil' Bazil..."

"It's not her son!"

"Exactly – so Babe – sit down..."

"Why?"

"'Cause you about to be mad..." Troy sat down and looked Keisha in the face... "I like Starr – but that Lil' Bitch told Beautiee you're not the only baby mother my father has..." Troy didn't say anything. He just sat there shakin' his head... "There's more..."

"What Keisha?"

"The Lil' Bitch goin' tell Beautiee this is not your house – this is my father's house..."

"You right – I'm mad – what did Bazil say?"

"First – Beautiee told her – see – that's where you fucked up – I'm not just his baby's mother – I'm his wife – then she got up, gave me the baby, and Bazil asked her where she was goin' – and Beautiee told him I'm going to put your daughter out of your house…"

"Oh shit! What Bazil do?"

"Bazil told Beautiee to close the door and come sit down and he told Starr to sit down…."

"Okay… I'm waiting…"

"First – he made Starr apologize – then he told her I love you with all my heart – but this is my wife – and this isn't my house – this is her house – and you didn't just hurt her – you hurt me…"

"Damn!"

"Right!"

"What happened after that?"

"She started crying…"

"Okay…"

"And Bazil told her save it – you can go now!" Keisha laughed…

"Oh shit! He put his daughter out?"

"Yes-the-fuck he did!"

"I love that mutha fucka too!" Troy laughed…

"She fucked up…"

"Hell yea!"

"Beautiee was so hurt…"

"How you know?"

"She was calm…"

"Oh shit…"

"I just hope she didn't take it out on Bazil – you know how she get when she gets mad…"

"I haven't heard anything since you came back so that means one of two things…"

"They not speakin' or they fuckin'!" Keisha laughed.

Chapter 16

"Hey Starr..." Chandler said as I closed the door and broke down crying...

"Starr... what's wrong?" he asked as he held me...

"I fucked up!" I cried...

"Shhh... It can't be that bad..."

"I really fucked up Chandler..."

"What happened?"

"I... I... Daddy..."

"Come sit down..." Chandler said as he led me to the couch... "I'm going to get us some wine..." Chandler said as he got up to get the wine. I watched him pour the glasses and come back to sit with me. As soon as he sat the glass down on the table I gulped it down... "Okay... tell me..."

"Keisha's planning a baby shower for Jay..."

"That's nice..."

"I said I was going to invite my mother..."

"Oh boy..."

"Beautiee said no the fuck you're not!"

"She didn't have to speak to you like that..."

"I know – so she tells Keisha about how she talked to Daddy for me to help my mother – I asked her what she's talkin' about – she tells me to stop playin' fuckin dumb!"

"See – I'ma have to talk to them – that's not right..."

"Then she tells Keisha I went crying to her when my mother called me a Lil' Bitch..."

"Why she bring that up?"

"Exactly! Then she tells Keisha she was mad when we went shopping for the wedding..."

"Was she?"

"She was mad at my mother... and I said something... so she got mad..."

"Okay... I get it..."

"Then she tells Keisha she saw my mother the other day and my mother told her if Jay was her son his name would be Lil' Bazil..."

"Now I understand – she wasn't really mad at you – she's mad at your mother – your mother doesn't know her place..."

"She's mad at me too... and so is my father..."

"What makes you say that?"

"Because..."

"What Starr?"

"I told her she's not the only baby mother my father has – and she told me I fucked up because she's not just his baby's mother – she's his wife..."

"Starr! Why would you say that to her?"

"Because my mother has a child with him too!"

"I understand how you feel Starr – but that was wrong..."

"I know..."

"Did you apologize?"

"Not right away..."

"Why not?"

"Beautiee said I wasn't inviting my mother to her house... and..."

"What?"

"I told her it's my father's house... not hers..."

"Starr!"

"I know, I know..."

"What happened?"

"Beautiee got up, opened the door, and told my father I'm putting your daughter out your house – but my father wouldn't let her..."

"That's good..."

"No it's not..."

"Why?"

"My father told me he loves me with all his heart – but Beautiee is his wife – and it's her house – and when I hurt her I also hurt him..."

"Damn..."

"I started crying... I told him I was sorry... and... he told me to leave!" I cried as Chandler held me...

Chapter 17

"Hey Keisha..." Beautiee said as she opened the door and let her in...

"You alright?"

"Yea.."

"You sure?"

"I'm good..."

"That was fucked up..."

"It was..."

"You and Bazil speaking?"

"Girl – we're trying to have another baby!" Beautiee laughed...

"Are you fuckin' serious?"

"Well... we're seriously fuckin'!" Beautiee laughed...

"I ain't mad – I'm just glad y'all are good..."

"We've been in a really good place since Jay was born – I love Bazil more than I did before I got pregnant..."

"See – that makes me happy – I'm glad that shit didn't bother you..."

"That shit broke my heart..."

"Damn Beautiee – I'm sorry..."

"I'm not - not anymore..."

"You're not?"

"Nope..."

"You still mad?"

"When I was pregnant – remember I told you I was tired?"

"Yea..."

"I did too much..."

"You right..."

"Now that Starr let me know I'm nothing but his baby's momma I'm going to be just that – his baby's momma – Starr has her own momma!" Beautiee laughed...

"Bazil gon' be okay with that?"

"He'll have to be..." Beautiee laughed...

"I hear that – are you really tryin' to have another baby though?"

"Well – we didn't wait for my six-week check-up – and we're not using protection... so..."

"Okay..." Keisha laughed... "But what if you get pregnant again?"

"Oh well..." Beautiee sighed...

"Whatever – I'm just glad you're happy..."

"Me too..."

"How's Bazil?"

"He cried..."

"After Starr said what she said?"

"No..."

"When then?"

"He cried when I told him I love him more..."

157

"Aww..."

"Don't get me wrong – I loved planning the wedding, booking the wedding, booking the honeymoon, the bed and breakfast... it was so romantic..."

"See – that made y'all fall in love again too..."

"It sure did... but now that it's over... I'm going to enjoy our son, finish my books, and be his wife..."

"Shit – that's plenty – especially if you're pregnant again..."

"Exactly!" Beautiee laughed...

"What if Starr gets pregnant? You planning a baby shower?"

"Hell no – that's her momma's job!" Beautiee laughed...

"You right..." Keisha laughed...

"Girl – you not gonna believe this one..."

"Oh God – what?"

"I told you I saw her the other day..."

"Yea..."

"It was at Dr. Julianne's office..."

"Y'all got the same gynecologist?"

"Yea..."

"Oh damn!"

"That's where she started that Lil' Bazil shit..."

"Whatchumean started?"

"Girl – we got on the elevator and we met the nicest couple..."

"Well that's nice..."

"It was – until Mary showed up in the cafeteria..."

"Oh Damn – what happened?"

"We met Chrissy and James – Chrissy runs a book club and they meet at her house every month..."

"Oh that's nice..."

"James treated us to brunch when he found out who Bazil was..."

"That was nice..."

"It was – he said he couldn't wait to tell the guys he met my husband..."

"That's nice..."

"Chrissy wants her book club to review my books so I'm giving her review copies..."

"That's nice..."

"So Mary comes into the cafeteria and Chrissy starts to introduce us..."

"Oh damn..."

"Mary joins us at the table..."

"Damn Beautiee..."

"She sits down and starts in with that Lil' Bazil bullshit again..."

"At the table? With James and Chrissy?"

"Yes..."

"Fuckin' Bitch..."

"So – again – Bazil tells her his name is Jay..."

"That's right..."

"The Bitch does it again..."

"You lyin'!"

"I wish I were – this time, Chrissy says Mr. Osgood specifically told you his name is Jay – why do you keep doing that?"

"What she say?"

"She said oh did I call him Lil' Bazil again? I'm sorry..." Beautiee answered as she mimicked her...

"Now I know why you went off on Starr..."

"I'm not done..."

"What the fuck?"

"So Chrissy's holding Jay and James asks if he's a good baby – Bazil says yes – this Bitch gon' say – well your daughter sure wasn't..."

"She was puttin' y'all on blast like that?"

"She thought she was..."

"She thought she was?"

"We told them we had a 22 year old daughter that just got married before Mary got there – but here's the best part..."

"What?"

"Mary's been talkin' about Starr at the book club for months..."

"Oh shit!"

"So before we leave, I take Jay from Chrissy – the Bitch gon' call him Lil' Bazil again..."

"She need her ass beat..."

"I told Bazil she was gonna make me kill her..."

"Okay Beautiee – I need you to take a deep breath..."

160

"Keisha – I'm good – it was just a moment..." Beautiee laughed...

"Starr doesn't know all this – does she?"

"No – and she won't..."

"You don't think you should tell her?"

"I think I should be her father's baby momma..."

"You right!" Keisha said as they both laughed...

Chapter 18

"Hi Mommy..." I said as I walked in...

"Starr!" my mother exclaimed as she hugged me... "How's married life?"

"Wonderful..."

"How's your father doing?" she asked as she closed the door...

"Mommy – I need tea..."

"Oh my God Starr – what happened?" I couldn't even answer – I just started crying. My mother didn't say anything – she just let me cry as she made tea for us and brought it to the table... "Drink your tea Starr..." she said as she picked up the cup, handed it to me, and I took a sip... "Now.... What happened?"

"Keisha's throwing Beautiee a baby shower..."

"Oh that's nice..."

"So I said I was gonna invite you..."

"Oh..."

"She says no-the-fuck you're not!"

"See – I'ma have to check her – I'on like that shit!"

"Then she's tellin' Keisha how she talked to Daddy so you could be here, she took us shopping for the wedding, and I went cryin' to her when you called me a Lil' Bitch..."

"I know what her problem is..."

"What Mommy?"

"She's mad because I told Bazil his son's name should be Lil' Bazil..."

"Mommy – he's not your son..."

"Doesn't matter – he's Bazil's first born – that child should be named after him..."

"Mommy – I got thrown out..."

"What?"

"I got thrown out!"

"By who?" Beautiee?"

"By Daddy..."

"Oh hell no – he's not gonna treat you like that – wait 'till I see his ass..."

"Mommy – he threw me out because of what I said..."

"What'd you say?"

"I told Beautiee she's not the only baby momma my father has..."

"I know that's right – my girl!" my mother said as she hugged me...

"Chandler said I was wrong to say that..."

"Why? 'Cause it's true?"

"Beautiee said I fucked up because she's not just his baby's momma – she's his wife..."

"Oh she's his wife – but she's his baby momma – and so am I – whether she likes it or not..."

"That's not all Mommy..."

"What else?"

"I told Beautiee this is my father's house – not yours..."

"So what? It is your father's house..."

"So Beautiee got up to put me out – but Daddy wouldn't let her..."

"Oh so your father does have good sense..."

"No Mommy..."

"What happened?'

"Daddy said he loves me with all his heart but Beautiee's his wife – it's her house – and when I hurt her I hurt him – then he told me to leave..."

"See – this is all because I told them his son should be named Lil' Bazil – I don't give a fuck what they say _ I'm not calling him Jay – I'm calling him Lil' Bazil..."

"Mommy! Stop it!" You'll just make it worse!" I cried...

"Okay Star – I'll stop – for you..."

"Thank you..."

"Le'me go get my mail..." my mother said as she went to get her mail. When she came back she put the mail down on the table and picked up an envelope, opened it, and started reading...

Hello Mary,

It was lovely seeing you the other day; however, I am writing to inform you that your

164

membership in the Vines Book Club has been revoked.

Before you came into the cafeteria, Mrs. Osgood offered to provide us with review copies of her book for our next monthly meeting. We are looking forward to a successful business relationship with the Osgoods and your behavior towards them the other day leads me to believe that having you as a member would jeopardize that.

Enclosed please find a check for partial reimbursement of your membership fee.

Sincerely,

Christine Vines

"Fuck y'all then!" my mother said as she put the check down on the table and tore up the letter...
"What's wrong Mommy?"
"Fuckin Bitch!"
"Mommy? What's wrong?"
"Beautiee got me kicked out the book club..."
"Mommy – Beautiee wouldn't do that..."
"Starr – Beautiee's not as nice as you think she is..."

"Yes she is – she's just mad… at you…"

"Well that's too fuckin' bad – she's gonna have to get over the fact that I have a child with her husband…"

"Mommy – she's not mad at you because of that…."

"Why she mad at me then?"

"She's mad at you because she knows you still want Daddy…"

"Starr!" I do not want your father!"

"Yes you do Mommy – I know it – and she knows it – that's why you said what you said…"

"What the fuck are you talkin' about?"

"You said if he was your son…"

"Yea I did – so what?"

"Mommy – you've always wanted Daddy – even when he was married to your best friend…"

"I wish I never laid eyes on your father…"

"You wanted him to marry you – didn't you?"

"Why the hell would you ask me that?"

"Didn't you?"

"Good bye Starr…"

"Oh so now you're throwing me out?"

"I can't throw you out your house Starr – but I'm ending this conversation – I'm going to lay down…" my mother said as she went into the bedroom.

Chapter 19

"Hello?" Beautiee answered...

"Hello Beautiee – it's Chrissy..."

"Hi Chrissy – how are you?"

"I'm fine – how's Jay?"

"He's just as happy as can be..."

"Oh I'm so glad to hear that – listen – I won't keep you – I just wanted to call and see if you got the information I sent you..."

"Yes – I got it yesterday – I'll get the books out to you on Monday..."

"Oh that's great – thank you – listen – we'd love to have you come do a reading... if it's not too much to ask..."

"I'd love to..."

"Oh wow – that's wonderful – thank you – the members will be so excited..."

"Yea – especially Mary..." Beautiee laughed...

"Mary won't be here..."

"She won't?"

"Mary's membership has been revoked..."

"Since when?"

"Since today..."

"Oh wow…"

"After our meeting in the cafeteria the other day I felt it was for the best…"

"Thank you Chrissy – I appreciate that…"

"You're welcome – we'll talk again soon – have a good day Beautiee…"

"You too Chrissy…" Beautiee said as she hung up…

"Who was that?" Bazil asked as he came into the office…

"That was Chrissy…"

"Oh – how is she?"

"She's fine – she wanted to know if I got her information – I'm going to have Joselyn send out the books on Monday…"

"Oh that's nice…"

"She wants me to come do a reading…"

"Are you going to?"

"Yes…"

"I'm sure Mary will love that…" Bazil laughed…

"Mary's membership was revoked…"

"Really?"

"Effective today…"

"Hmmm… musta been something she said…" Bazil said as they both laughed… "Jay's asleep…" Bazil said as he came up behind Beautiee, pulled her to him, held her, and kissed her on her neck…

"He is?" Beautiee breathed…

"We could go upstairs…" he said as he turned her around and kissed her fully…

"We could..." Beautiee breathed...

"Do you remember what you said in the hospital?"

"I remember..."

"Let's do it now..."

"Okay..." Bazil took Beautiee by the hand and led her upstairs to the bedroom. When they got in the bedroom Beautiee took off her clothes and jumped on the bed...

"What's the hurry?" Bazil laughed...

"Hurry up..." Beautiee said...

"Say please..."

"Please... before Jay wakes up..."

"Okay..." Bazil laughed as he took off his clothes and came up to the head of the bed...

"Wait..." Beautiee said...

"Make up your mind..." Bazil laughed...

"I just want to look at you..." Bazil stood there and stroked himself while Beautiee watched...

"Is this what you want?"

"Yes... that's what I want..." Bazil came over to the bed, crawled up over her head, and tapped his dick on her mouth. Beautiee opened her mouth slightly, took the head in her mouth, and started licking the head of his dick. Bazil enjoyed what she was doing and what he was feeling as well as watching her enjoy what she was doing until she lifted her head up and took more of his dick in her mouth. Bazil laid down on top of her, spread her legs, spread her lips with is tongue, and started sucking her clit as she

169

grabbed his ass and pushed his dick further into her mouth... "Mmmph... Mmmph... Mmmph... Mmmph..."

"Hmmm... Hmmm... Hmmm... Hmmm..." Beautiee was coming all over herself and Bazil was licking her pussy all over sucking her juices as he continued fucking her mouth...

"Mmmph... Mmmph... Mmmph... Mmmph..."

"Hmmm... Hmmm... Hmmm... Hmmm..." Willlie's body was shaking and Beautiee held him down by his ass so he'd stay in her mouth as he came...

"Mmmph! Mmmph! Mmmph! Mmmph! Mmmmpppphhhh!!!" Beautiee swallowed and continued sucking as Bazil grabbed her legs and held them tight as he licked and sucked on her clit...

"Hmmm! Hmmm! Hmmm! Hmmm! Hmmmmmmm!!!" Bazil held her down as her body shook beneath him and just as her orgasm subsided he put his arms under her, held her, and flipped her over so that he was underneath her and she was on top of him, just like she wanted, and they continued licking and sucking each other...

"Mmmph... Mmmph... Mmmph... Mmmph..."

"Hmmm... Hmmm... Hmmm... Hmmm..."
"Mmmph... Mmmph... Mmmph... Mmmph..."

"Hmmm... Hmmm... Hmmm... Hmmm..."
"Mmmph... Mmmph... Mmmph... Mmmph..."

"Hmmm... Hmmm... Hmmm... Hmmm..."

"Mmmph... Mmmph... Mmmph... Mmmph..."

"Hmmm... Hmmm... Hmmm... Hmmm..."

"Mmmmpppphhhh!!!"

"Hmmmmmmm!!!" Bazil turned them both on their side and they continued licking and sucking each other until they heard Jay.

Chapter 20

"Hey Chan..." I said as I came in and closed the door...

"Hey Starr..." Chandler said as he pulled me into a kiss and held me...

"Mmmm... That was nice..."

"I can be nicer..." Chandler said as he started kissing me on my neck..."

"Ooohhh... that's nice too..."

"I can be even nicer..." Chandler said as he held me and walked me backwards into the bedroom...

"Just how nice can you be?" I asked as he led me to the bed...

"Depends on what you tell me..."

"Tell you?"

"Starr?"

"Yes Chandler?"

"Do you have something you need to tell me?"

"You found them – didn't you?"

"Yes – I found them..." Chandler answered as he kissed me...

"I... was... going... to tell... you..." I said between kisses...

"How... late... are... you?"

"I... haven't... had... my period... in about... two months..."

"So... Mrs. Corbett... it's possible... you... got... pregnant... the first night... we... made... love... is... that... what... you're... telling... me?"

"Yes..."

"Here..."Chandler said as he handed me one of the pregnancy tests... "Go find out..."

"Okay..." I said as I got up and smiled at him... "I'll be right back..." I said as I went into the bathroom, opened the pregnancy test, sat on the toilet, peed, and waited...

"You okay Starr?"

"Yes Chandler... I'm okay..." I started crying as soon as I saw the results...

"You sure you're okay Starr? You sound like you're crying..."

"Chandler..." I whispered as I came out the bathroom holding the pregnancy test. Chandler came over to me, took the test from me, saw the results, and started crying...

"Oh my God... Starr... we're having a baby?"

"Yes Chandler... We're having a baby..."

"We're having a baby!" Chandler yelled as he picked me up off the floor and spun me around...

"Yes... we're having a baby..." I said as Chandler put me back down and kissed me hard...

"I love you so much..."

"I love you too..."

"C'mon..." Chandler said as he grabbed my hand and pulled me towards the front door...

"Where are we going?" I laughed...

"Charles and Theresa..." Chandler answered as he opened our door and banged on their door...

"Who is it?" Charles asked...

"Chandler!"

"Hey Chandler – everything okay?"

"Who is it honey?" Theresa asked as she came to the door... "Oh hi! Come in - Charles – let them in!" Theresa laughed...

"Sorry about that..." Charles laughed as he opened the door... "It's nice to see you – we haven't had a chance to talk since you've been back from your honeymoon- how was it?"

"Bermuda was wonderful..." I sighed...

"That it was... that it was..." Chandler answered...

"Listen – we were just about to have dinner..."

"Oh – my bad – we'll come back..." Chandler said...

"Chandler! Sit Down!" Charles laughed...

"Okay... thank you..." Chandler said...

"You drinkin' Chandler?" Charles asked...

"Hell yea! Whatchu got?"

"I got Henney..."

"Okay!" Chandler laughed...

"We'll have wine Starr..." Theresa said...

"I don't know if I should..."

"Why?" Theresa asked. I didn't answer her – I just sat there smiling...

"Oh my God – you're pregnant!" Theresa yelled as she grabbed me into a hug...

"Yes – I'm pregnant!"

"Oh man – congratulations!" Charles said as he poured drinks and offered Chandler his glass...

"Thank ya, thank ya..." Chandler said as he took a gulp and set down the empty glass...

"Starr – you can have a little wine – it won't hurt the baby..." Theresa said...

"Are you sure?"

"Yes Starr – besides – I'm a lightweight – there's only 8 percent alcohol in here..." she laughed as she poured us both a glass of wine and handed me a glass...

"Ohhh... this is sweet..." I said as I sipped it...

"It's one of my favorites..." Theresa said...

"What's for dinner?" I asked...

"Spaghetti..."

"Ohh... that sounds delicious..." I said...

"It is – especially when my wife makes it..." Charles said...

"Aww... thank you baby..." Theresa said as she went over to Charles and kissed him...

"So when did you find out you were pregnant?" Theresa asked...

"We just found out..." Chandler answered...

"You just found out?" and you told us first?" Charles asked...

"Yea..."

"Aww shit – we special!" Charles laughed...

"I couldn't wait to tell somebody!" Chandler laughed...

"What about your family? Don't you want to tell them?" Theresa asked...

"We can tell them later..." I sighed...

"Chandler – let's go out on the balcony and have a cigar while we wait for dinner..." he said as he got up...

"Okay..." Chandler laughed as he followed Charles outside...

"I'm glad you're so happy..." Theresa said...

"Me too..." I said...

"I need to tell you something..."

"Okay..."

"You saved our marriage..."

"We did?"

"Yea..."

"Aww..." I said as I went to give her a hug...

"I kinda shut down... we stopped making love... at one point I wanted to divorce him..."

"Oh wow..."

"When we heard you on the balcony it changed everything..."

"So... you're having sex again?"

"Girllll – we've been fuckin' non-stop!" she laughed...

"I'm so happy for you..."

"Me too girl – le'me check on the spaghetti..." she said as she went to check on it and came back...

"It's ready – we can eat outside on the deck if you want..."

"I kinda like sitting in here talkin' to you – you're the only friend I have..."

"Aww... thank you – I like having you as a friend too – let me make plates for the guys – I'll be right back..."

"Okay..." I watched her make the plates and take them out to Chandler and Charles...

"Hi guys – here's your dinner..." Theresa said...

"Thank you baby..." Charles said...

"Thank you Theresa – where's Starr?"

"She's inside..."

"Is she coming out here?"

"No – we're gonna stay inside and talk..."

"Okay..." Chandler said as Theresa came back inside...

"Hey – I'm back – I'll get us plates..."

"Okay..." I sighed...

"You okay Starr?"

"Yea..." I sighed. I watched Theresa make us plates and bring them to the table...

"Taste it..." Theresa said as she gave me a fork...

"Oh my God! This is so good! You have to show me how to make this!"

"Maybe..." Theresa laughed as we ate... "So... let's talk... are you sure you're okay?"

"I'm really hapy..." I answered as I started crying...

"Starr... what's wrong?"

"I love Chandler so much... I told him I wanted to have his children... and now I'm pregnant..."

"Aww... I'm glad you're so happy..."

"I am..."

"Whatcha think of my wife's spaghetti?" Charles asked as the guys came inside...

"It's delicious..." I answered...

"I told you!" Charles laughed...

"You ready Starr?" Chandler asked...

"Ready?"

"Yea... ready..." Chandler answered as he smiled at me mischievously...

"Yes Chandler..." I'm ready..." I answered as I smiled back at him...

"Thanks for dinner and drinks – we got next – but we gotta go now..." Chandler said as he came over to me, took me by the hand, and led me towards the door...

"Thanks for dinner and the wine – bye..." I laughed as Chandler opened the door, pulled me out the door, closed it, pulled me to our door, opened it, pulled me inside, closed the door, pushed me up against it, and put his tongue in my mouth...

"Mmmmm...." I moaned. Chandler pulled me to him, held me, and continued kissing me as he started walking me backwards towards the bedroom. When we got in the bedroom Chandler undressed me completely and then he spoke...

"Don't move..."

"Okay..." I breathed. Chandler got down on his knees in front of me and began kissing and licking my pussy as I stood there... "Chandler... Chandler..." I moaned as Chandler grabbed my ass, pushed me towards him, and devoured me... "Chandler... Ooohhhh... Chandler... Huuhhh... Huuhhh... Huuhhh..." I grabbed Chandler's head with both hands and held his head as I started trembling... "Huuhhh... Huuhhh... Huuhhh... Chandler... I'm cumming... Haaahhh... Haaahhh... Haaaaahhhhhh!"

"Oh my God – is that Starr?" Theresa asked..."

"Yes..." Charles answered...

"Damn – I didn't know my spaghetti was that good..." she laughed...

"You know..." Charles said as he pulled Theresa to him... "As long as we're listening to them..." he said as he started kissing her neck... "We might as well join them..."

"Okay..." Charles undressed Theresa, took her by the hand, and led her to the bedroom...

Chandler looked up at me and started crying... "Chandler..." I whispered as I stood there and held his head... "What's wrong?"

"I love you..."

"I love you too..." Chandler stood up, took my face in his hands, and kissed me...

"Mmmm...." I moaned...

"It's good... isn't it?" Chandler asked as we continued kissing...

"Yes..." I breathed as he put his tongue in my mouth so I could suck it...

"Get on the bed and get on your back..."

"Okay..."

Charles got down on his knees in front of Theresa, grabbed her ass, pushed her towards his mouth, and started licking and sucking her pussy... "Oh Charles... it's been so long..."

I watched Chandler undress completely and then he climbed up on the bed between my legs and laid on my stomach...

"Oh Charles... Oh God... Charles... Don't stop... Yes... Yes..."

"Is that Theresa?" I asked...

"Yes... Chandler answered...

"Charles... I'm cumming... I'm cumming... Aaaaggghhhh!"

180

"I wonder if they heard us? I was kinda loud..." I laughed...

"You were..." Chandler laughed...

"I couldn't help it... it felt so good..."

"It's gonna be like that..."

"It is?"

"You're pregnant – you're gonna be horny – and you'll come... a lot..."

"I will?"

"And..." he said as he started kissing his way up my stomach... "When you come... it will be intense..."

"Oooohhh..."

"And..." he said as he started sucking my left breast... "These... mmmm... will be nice... soft... and... your milk... will be... sweet..."

"Ohhh... that feels good..."

"Can't forget this one..." Chandler said as he started sucking the right one...

"Oh... Chandler..."

"Yes Starr?" Chandler breathed as he eased himself inside me...

"Get on the bed... and get on your back..." Charles told Theresa...

"Okay..."

"Chandler..." I moaned as he started thrusting...

"Your pussy... is... ohh... shit... damn... ummph..."

"Is it good... Chandler?"

"Hell yea... ummph..."

"Ooohhh... is it because... I'm... pregnant... huh..."

"No... you... always... had... good... pussy... umph..."

"Ooohhh... Chandler.... Chandler... Yes..."

"Charles... Yes..."

"Ugh! Fuck!"

"Charles... Ohh... Yes..."

"You want this dick... don't you?"

"Yes Charles... Yes..."

"Say it..."

"I want your dick!"

"And... I want... your... pussy... ugh!"

Chandler picked up my legs, put them on his shoulders, and fucked me deeper... "Oh... Chandler... Oh God... It feels so good... I'm cummmiiinnnggg!"

Charles picked up Theresa's legs, put them on his shoulders, and fucked her deeper... "Charles... Oh God! Fuck me! Yes! Yes! Aaaaggghhh!"

"Starr... Ummph! Ummph! Ummph! Ummph! Uuuummmmmppphhhh!!"

"Theresa... Uggh! Uggh! Uggh! Uggh! Uuuugggghhhh!!!"

Chandler put my legs down, laid down on top of me, and kissed me... "Oh my God... that was so good..." I breathed...

"Yes... it was..."

"I'm so happy Chandler..."

"So am I..." he said as we continued kissing...

Charles put Theresa's legs down, laid on top of her, and kissed her... "Charles... I love you..."

"I love you too..."

"Oh my God... that was so good..."

"It was..."

"I missed you..."

"I missed you too..." he said as they continued kissing.

Chapter 21

"Good morning Chandler..." my father answered...

"Good morning Daddy..." Chandler laughed...

"How's everything?"

"Absolutely wonderful..."

"Aww... I'm glad to hear that Chandler..."

"Hi Chandler!" Beautiee yelled in the background...

"Good morning Beautiee..." Chandler said...

"Chandler says good morning..." my father said to Beautiee as she fed Jay...

"Listen – I'm taking you to breakfast on Sunday – Cracker Barrel – how early do you get up?" Chandler asked...

"Beautiee – how early does Jay get us up for breakfast?" my father asked...

"Between 7 and 8..."

"Beautiee says between 7 and 8..."

"Okay – meet us there as close to 8 as you can – we'll be there already – I like to get a good table..." Chandler said...

"Who's us?" my father asked...

"If I tell you – you promise you'll still come?"

"Mary's gonna be there – isn't she?" my father laughed...

"Yes..."

"Sure Chandler – we'll see you Sunday at Cracker Barrel – 8 am or shortly thereafter..." my father said as Chandler hung up...

"We're all set for Sunday morning at Cracker barrel – we'll pick your mother up and go straight there..."

"Beutiee's coming too – right?" I asked...

"Your father said they'll be there..."

"They know my mother's gonna be there – and they're still coming?"

"Yea..."

"Aww... I'm so happy!" I squealed as I jumped into Chandler's arms...

"I'm happy too – I can't wait to tell them..." Chandler said as he kissed me...

"I can't wait either!"

"Starr – don't you dare!"

"I'm not!"

"You promise?"

"Yes Chandler – I promise!" I laughed...

"Thank God we told Charles and Theresa..."

"I know! I'm glad you told them – it felt so good to say it out loud!"

"That's not the only thing that felt good..." Chandler said as he pulled me to him and put his tongue in my mouth...

"Mmmm.... Chandler..." I moaned as we held each other, tonguing each other down...

"What's happening on Sunday?" Beautiee asked...

"Chandler's treating us to breakfast...

"Hmmm... that's nice – we're not bringing Jay..."

"Why not?"

"I'm not sitting through what happened the other day every time we see Mary – not that I want to see her anyway..."

"Would you rather stay home?"

"No – I'll go – I'm not mad with Chandler..."

"I'm not either – but they'll ask to see Jay..."

"I'm sorry Bazil – I can't do it – please don't ask me to..."

"Come here..." Bazil said as he went over to Beautiee, pulled her into a hug, and kissed her...

"I love you..."

"I love you too..."

"So you're okay if we don't bring Jay?"

"Honestly?"

"Yea..."

"No..."

"I'm sorry..."

"So am I..."

"We can bring him..." Beautiee sighed...

"It's fine – it'll be our first time away from him – but we're only going around the corner so we'll be close by..."

"I wish Mary wasn't gonna be there..."

"So do I..."

"Chandler's up to something..."

"What makes you so sure?"

"He's inviting all of us to breakfast..."

"That means he's up to something?"

"Yes..."

"Hmmm.... you're probably right..."

"Maybe we'll be too full to start anything..."

"I hope so..."

"I hope so too – I'ma call Keisha right now..."

"Right now?"

"Yea..."

"You sure you wanna do that?"

"Why?"

"It's kinda early..."

"Bazil – it's after 8..."

"Okay..." Bazil laughed...

"Hu... hello?" Keisha answered...

"Damn – I'm sorry – I didn't mean to wake you..."

"That's okay – you good?"

"Yea..."

"You sure?"

"Can y'all watch Jay on Sunday?"

"Troy – get up!"

"Why?"

"Beautiee wants us to watch Jay on Sunday..."

"Oh shit – wai' a min – le'me go to the bathroom..." Troy said as he got up, went to the bathroom, and came back... "Okay – I'm back now – what's goin' on?"

"Well..." Beautiee sighed...

"I knew it!" Keisha laughed...

"So... Chandler invited us to breakfast..."

"On Sunday?"

"Yea..."

"Where y'all goin'?"

"Cracker Barrel..."

"Shit – I wanna go!" Keisha laughed...

"Why don't you wanna bring Jay?"

"I don't want my son anywhere near Mary..."

"Aaah shit – Mary's gonna be there – Chandler's up to something!"

"That's what I told Bazil..."

"He's okay with y'all not bringing Jay?"

"No..."

"Damn Beautiee..."

"I know... but I just can't..."

"I know girl – what the hell you gonna do when he gets older? You can't avoid Mary forever..."

"Girl – I'ma try!" Beautiee laughed...

"Tell Bazil we'll take good care of Jay!" Troy yelled...

188

"They know that Troy – shut up!" Keisha laughed...

"I just can't sit there and listen to Lil' Bazil this, Lil' Bazil that, his name should be Lil' Bazil..."

"Yo – why don't she shut the fuck up? He's not her son!" Troy yelled...

"Because she wish he was..." Beautiee answered...

"You really believe that?" Keisha asked...

"I know it..."

"Damn..."

"Why else would she care so much?"

"You right..."

Chapter 22

"Good afternoon..." Mary said as she answered the phone...

"May I speak with Mary Smith please?"

"Speaking..."

"Ms. Smith, this is John Herrington, Director, Office of the State Comptroller, Retirement Services Division for the State of Connecticut..."

"Hello Mr. Herrington – how may I help you?"

"We received information from the Connecticut State Retirement System regarding Officer Jermoll Thompson..."

"Okay..."

"It seems that, according to their records, Officer Thompson recently passed away..."

"Yes – that's correct – but what does this have to do with me?"

"Well – I'm glad you asked – whenever there's money that hasn't been collected, this office is contacted to track down the beneficiary..."

"Are you telling me Jermoll named me beneficiary?"

"That's exactly what I'm telling you..."

"Oh wow! We were engaged to be married..."

"I'm very sorry for your loss..."

"Thank you..."

"Listen – take this phone number..."

"Okay – hold on..." she said as she went to get pen and paper... "Okay – I'm ready..."

"1-860-702-3480 – press option 5 – then follow the prompts..."

"Okay..."

"You can also email them at osc.rsd@ctgov..."

"Thank you so much for calling me!"

"You're welcome Ms. Smith – you can file for benefits on the phone or you can go to the local office Downtown Bridgeport..."

"How soon will I get the first check?"

"It usually takes 30 days..."

"Okay – thank you again..."

"You're welcome Ms. Smith – have a good afternoon..."

"Thank you – same to you!"

"Hi Mommy..."

"Starr – I know you're busy – but guess what?"

"What Mommy?"

"Jermoll made me the beneficiary on his retirement benefits!"

"Oh wow – that's nice…"

"He really loved me…"

"I'm happy for you Mommy…"

"Starr?"

"Yes Mommy?"

"You okay?"

"I'm fine…"

"You're lying!"

"Mommy – I have to go now…"

"What's going on Starr?"

"We're having sex – bye!"

"Why'd you tell her that?" Chandler laughed…

"I didn't know what else to say!" I laughed…

"Damn Starr – you can't answer the phone again until Monday!" Chandler laughed…

"She said Jermoll made her the beneficiary on his retirement benefits…"

"Oh shit! Your mother's about to get paid!"

"Really?"

"Starr – Jermoll died in the line of duty – his pension will be higher – she's gonna get about $2,000 a month…"

"Oh wow! I'ma call her back…"

"No…"

"No?"

"No…"

"You're right – I can't be trusted…" I laughed…

"Let your mother find out when she gets the paperwork – they'll tell her whatever it is…

"Okay..."

"Hi Mary..." Chandler said as Mary walked into the precinct...

"Hi Chandler – I'm here to see..."

"I know – go down the hall – last door on the right..."

"Okay – thanks..." Mary said as she walked down the hall to Mr. Jenkin's office... "Mr. Jenkins?"

"Mary Smith?"

"Yes – I'm Mary Smith..."

"Come in – please – have a seat..."

"Thank you..." Mary said as she sat down in front of Mr. Jenkins..."

"Okay Mary – I need to see some ID before we do anything..."

"Here..." Mary said as she took her ID out of her purse and put it on the table...

"Okay – just sign where I've indicated on these forms..."

"Okay..." Mary squealed as she signed the papers...

"Okay – I'll be right back..." Mr. Jenkins said as he took the papers and went into another room. When he came back he handed Mary an envelope...

"What's this?" Mary asked...

"Your check..."

"Do I have to come down here every month?"

"Ms. Smith – you don't understand..."

"What don't I understand?"

"Jermoll took out a loan for $50,000 before he died – that loan wasn't repaid..."

"Okay – so I can't get a reduced benefit?"

"Ms. Smith – when you take out a loan against your pension and it's not repaid – the pension amount is reduced by $100 for every thousand borrowed – that check I gave you is all that's left..."

"So I'm not getting any more checks?"

"No... I'm sorry..."

"Well – thank you for this one..." Mary said as she got up to leave...

"You're welcome – have a good day..."

"You too..." Mary said as she stopped to open the envelope and saw the amount of the check for $5,000..."

"Fuckin' greedy Bitch..." someone said as they peeked around the corner.

Chapter 23

"Good morning Amy..." I sang as I walked into work..."

"Uh huh..." Amy replied as she looked me up and down...

"Is something wrong?" I asked...

"Honey – you're not fooling me one bit..."

"Amy – what'd I do?"

"Starr..." Amy laughed... "Stop..."

"Stop what?"

"Honey – I know..."

"Oh my God! Who told you?"

"Honey..." Amy laughed... "The way you walked in here just now – glowing and singing..." Amy laughed... "You're pregnant!"

"Yes... I'm pregnant..." I whispered as I started crying...

"Aww..." Amy said as she got up to hug me...

"I'm sorry..."

"Honey – as long as you're happy – you can cry all you want..."

"I can't help it – I'm so happy..."

"I know – I was the same way..."

"You were?"

"Yea…"

"Are you and your son close?"

"Yea – we have a great relationship…"

"Aww… I want that…"

"So… do you want a boy or a girl?"

"I want one… or two… of each…"

"Wow! How does Chandler feel about that?"

"He wants children too…"

"Aww… you're going to make great parents…"

"Really? You think so?"

"I know so…"

"Thank you Amy…"

"Have you told your parents yet?"

"No…"

"Why not?"

"We're waiting until Sunday…"

"Oh okay… tell them all at once…"

"Yea…"

"Starr? Are you okay?"

"I guess…"

"No you're not – talk to me…"

"I just want us all to get along…"

"All of you… or your two mothers?"

"How'd you know?"

"Honey – I've been there…"

"Really? How'd you do it?"

"Honey – I never did it…"

"Never?"

"When my son is around – I'm cordial – if wasn't for him – I wouldn't even deal with the Bitch!"

"You sound like Beautiee..."

"Honey – I am Beautiee..."

"It makes me sad..."

"C'mere Starr..." she said as she pulled me into a hug... "I'm sorry you're caught in the middle – but as long as your mother still loves your father – it's going to be a problem..."

"How did you know that?"

"I told you – I've been there..."

"Why can't my mother move on?"

"Because her heart won't let her..."

"She was engaged to Officer Thompson..."

"She was?"

"Yea..."

"Aww... now I understand – that makes it even worse..."

"I don't know what to do..."

"Sweetie – you can't do anything – the only thing you can do is love your husband..."

"I do – but I love my father and my mother too..."

"I know you do – but you have to let them work this out – you can't take it on..."

"It's hard..."

"Tell ya what – every time you start to feel down – go online and look at all the things you can buy for your baby..."

"I'm already doing that..." I laughed...

"It makes you happy – right?"

"Yes…"

"Good – that's your job for the duration of your pregnancy – you are to do whatever makes you happy – understand?"

"Yes Maam…" I laughed…

"Did you just call me Maam?"

"Sorry… yes Amy…"

"That's better…"

Chapter 24

"Bazil... Bazil..." Beautiee moaned...

"Ummph... Ummph... Ummph... Ummph..."

"Huhh... Huhh... Huhh... Huhh..." Bazil stopped, pulled out, got up on his knees, looked down at Beautiee, and smiled...

"Turn around... get on your knees... and grab the head board..." he commanded...

"Okay..." Beautiee breathed as she did as she was told...

"Spread your legs for me...."

"Okay..." Bazil reached between Beautiee's legs and her legs were shaking. Bazil came up behind Beautiee, held her against him, and ran his hands up and down her body as he breathed on her neck...

"Bazil... please..."

"Please what?"

"Please... fuck me..."

"I will..." he breathed in her ear as he bit her ear lobe... "In a bit..."

"Oh God... Bazil..." Beautiee moaned as Bazil massaged her breasts..."

"Yes... Beautiee..." he breathed in her ear as he moved his hands down her body...

"Please..."

"I'm enjoying this..." Bazil breathed in her ear as he pushed the tip of his dick inside her...

"Ooohhh..." she moaned...

"Uh uh... not yet..." he breathed as he spread her lips with his right hand and started playing with her clit...

"Ohh... Bazil... Fuck..."

"Uh uh... not yet..." he breathed as he eased the rest of his dick inside her while continuing to play with her clit...

"Bazil... please... fuck me... I can't take it..."

"I love it when you beg for my dick..." he said as he started thrusting slowly..."

"Oh shit... fuck me..."

"You want more?" he asked as he tortured her with long, slow strokes, pulling all the way out, and easing himself all the way back in while continuing to play with her clit..."

"Yes! Oh God! I'm cumming! Fuck me!"

"Now..." he said as he started slamming his dick inside her... "I'll fuck you..."

"Oh God! Bazil! Don't stop!"

"I won't! Uggh! Uggh! Uggh! Uggh!"

"Ahhh! Ahhh! Ahhh! Ahhh! Aaaahhhhhh!"

"Uggh! Uggh! Uggh! Uggh! Uuuuggghhhh!" Beautiee let go of the head board and collapsed onto the bed with Bazil on top of her, still inside her...

"How much time do we have before Jay wakes up?" Beautiee breathed...

"The way your breasts feel..." he breathed in her ear as he nibbled on her earlobe... "We don't have much time..."

"Can I have some more? Please?"

"You want more?" Bazil asked as he started thrusting...

"Yes..."

"Mmmm... okay..."

"Ooohhh..."

"Get on your back..."

"Okay..." Beautiee breathed as she flipped over and spread her legs..."

"Yeeessss..." Beautiee moaned as Bazil started fucking her again...

"We'll have to make... this... quick... uggh!"

"I don't care..." Beautiee said as she pulled Bazil down on top of her, took his face in her hands, and put her tongue in his mouth. Bazil covered her mouth with his and tongued her down fiercely as he fucked her...

"Ummph... Ummph... Ummph... Ummph..."

"Mmmm..... Mmmm..... Mmmm..... Mmmm....."

"Ummph... Ummph... Ummph... Ummph..."

"Mmmm..... Mmmm..... Mmmm..... Mmmm....."

"Ummph... Ummph... Ummph... Ummph... Uuuummmmpppphhhhh!!"

"Mmmm..... Mmmm..... Mmmm..... Mmmm..... Mmmmmmmmmmm!! It's... so... quiet..." Beautiee whispered between kisses...

"That's... a good... thing..." Bazil breathed...

"I wonder if Jay's awake?"

"You want me to go check on him?"

"Yea – we need to get ready anyway..."

"Okay..." Bazil said as he got up and went to get Jay... "Well good morning!" Bazil said when he saw Jay...

"Good morning Daddy..." Jay cooed... Jay looked at Bazil and smiled the biggest smile...

"How long have you been awake anyway?" Bazil asked as he picked Jay up and brought him into the bedroom to Beautiee...

"Good morning Jay..." Beautiee said as she took him from Bazil...

"Good morning Mommy – I gave you a minute - just like you asked me to..." Jay cooed...

"I wonder what he's saying?" Bazil asked...

"Judging by the way he's sucking my titty – he's probably saying 'bout damn time – I was hungry!" Beautiee laughed...

"We need to get ready..."

"I know – go get me the breast pump so I can make a couple of bottles for Jay..."

"You have enough milk for that?"

"Yea – besides – I only need to make two four-ounce bottles..."

"Okay – I'll be right back..." Bazil said as he went to get the breast pump. When he came back, Beautiee waited for Jay to finish before she started using the pump...

"Does it hurt?"

"No..."

"What's it feel like?"

"It doesn't feel as good as you..." Beautiee sighed...

"I'm sorry..." Bazil said as he sat down on the bed and began massaging her back...

"All done – now we can get ready – put these bottles in that bag over there with his diapers and change of clothes..."

"Okay..."

"Okay Jay – Mommy and Daddy need to get dressed – we're gonna put you back in your room – then we'll come get you..." Beautiee said as she got up and took Jay back to his room. When Beautiee came back into the bedroom, Bazil was standing there smiling, fully erect... "Damn Bazil – we can't..." she said as she went over to him and he pulled her close to him...

"So..." he said as he started kissing her... "What you're saying is... you don't want this dick?"

"C'mon –let's get in the shower and get dressed..." Beautiee breathed as she snatched Bazil by the hand, pulled him into the shower, and turned on the water. Bazil didn't wait a minute – he pushed Beautiee up against the wall, Beautiee grabbed the supports, Bazil picked up her legs, wrapped them around him, and started pounding... "Bazil! Bazil! Fuck!"

"Ugh! Ugh! Ugh! Ugh! Ugh! Ugh!"

"Ahh! Ahh! Ahh! Ahh! Ahh! Ahh!"

"Uuuuuugggghhhh!"

"Aaaaahhhhhhh!"

"Damn..." Bazil breathed as he kissed her...

"We need to get ready..."

"Jay's fine..." Bazil breathed as he kissed her again...

"It's already... after... 8..." Beautiee said between kisses...

"Okay... you're lucky... we have... to be... somewhere..."

"I know..."

"Okay – let's do this..."

"Okay..." Once they washed and got out the shower, Beautiee went to get Jay dressed and ready...

"You ready Beautiee?" Bazil called from downstairs...

"I'm on my way downstairs..." Beautiee said as she came downstairs with Jay and they headed to Troy and Keisha's house...

"'Bout time y'all got here – give me the baby..." Keisha said as she took him...

"Well good morning to you too..." Bazil laughed...

"Good morning – and good bye – see y'all later..." she said as she opened the door for us to leave...

"Damn Keisha – did you say hello before you put them out?" Troy laughed...

"Yes... she did..." Beautiee laughed...

"Keisha?"

"Yes Bazil?"

"There's two bottles, some diapers, and a change of clothes..."

"Okay Bazil – I got this – go!"

"Okay..." Bazil laughed...

"Bye Jay – we'll be back later..." Bazil said as he kissed Jay on the forehead... and Jay started crying...

"Uh uh – don't start that – they'll be back later – hush Jay..." Keisha said...

"C'mere Jay..." Beautiee said as she took Jay from Keisha... "Mommy and Daddy are going out for a little while – we'll be back – you'll be fine..." she said as she kissed Jay... and he started crying again...

"Oh boy... maybe we should..." Bazil started to say...

"Maybe we should just go ahead – he'll be alright – they got him – see you later – y'all want us to bring you back anything?"

"Naa... go 'head – we'll see you later..." Troy said as he closed the door... and Jay started screaming...

"No Bazil..." Beautiee said...

"Are you sure?"

"No..."

"You wanna go get him?"

"No..." Beautiee whispered with tears in her eyes... "He'll be fine..."

"You sure?"

"Bazil – it's his first time away from us – we need to leave him sooner or later – it's not like we can't trust them..."

"You right – let's go have breakfast..." Bazil said as they went to get in the car...

"You owe me $10..." Troy laughed...

"Aiight! Damn!" Keisha laughed as she handed Troy $10..."

"I told you they wouldn't come back in here..." Troy laughed...

"Okay... you right – but they thought about it..."

"They did – they stayed outside the door for a minute..." Troy laughed...

"See Troy – he laughing too – he aiight – right Jay?" Keisha said as she picked him up out the car seat and started playing with him.

"Oh God – I'm so nervous..." Beautiee said after they got out the car...

"Why?"

"I just want to have a nice breakfast..."

"Come here..." Bazil said as he took Beautiee in his arms and held her...

"Yes... My Thirst Quencher?" she answered as she looked up at him...

"That..." he said and then he kissed her... "That right there..." he said and then he kissed her again... "Is where you need to be - I'm right here..."

"Okay..."

"Will y'all come inside already?" Chandler laughed...

"Hi Chandler..." Bazil laughed... "We're comin'"

"Hi Chandler – sorry..." Beautiee laughed as they all walked inside to the table...

"Daddy! I said as I got up to hug my father...

"Good morning Starr..." he said as he hugged me...

"I guess I don't get one..." Beautiee sighed...

"Hi Beautiee..." I said as I gave her a hug...

"Good morning Starr..." she said as she hugged me back... "Good morning Mary..." Beautiee said as she sat down next to my mother...

"Good morning..." my mother said without looking up...

"Okay..." Beautiee said...

"Good morning Mary..." my father said as he sat down next to Beautiee...

"Good morning..." my mother said without looking up at my father...

"Okay – I'm just gonna say this right quick – we're pregnant!" Chandler said...

"Oh my God! Yes!" Beautiee said as she jumped up, pulled me up outta my seat, and hugged me tight..."

"Thank you..." I laughed...

"Chandler – oh my God – congratulations!" Beautiee laughed as she tried to pull him up out of his seat but couldn't... "Will you get up so I can give you a hug dammit!" she laughed...

"Okay..." Chandler laughed...

"Congratulations..." my father said as he pulled me into a hug... and then he started crying...

"Daddy? Are you okay?"

"Yes... I'm just happy..."

"Aww... I love you Daddy..."

"I love you too..."

"Do you love me Daddy?" Chandler laughed... "She wouldn't be pregnant if it wasn't for me..."

"Yes Chandler – I love you too..." my father laughed as he hugged Chandler...

"Congratulations Mary – you're going to be a grandma..." Beautiee said...

"Yes... yes I am – and since you said that – we need to establish some rules..."

<u>Twisted Starr Tree</u>

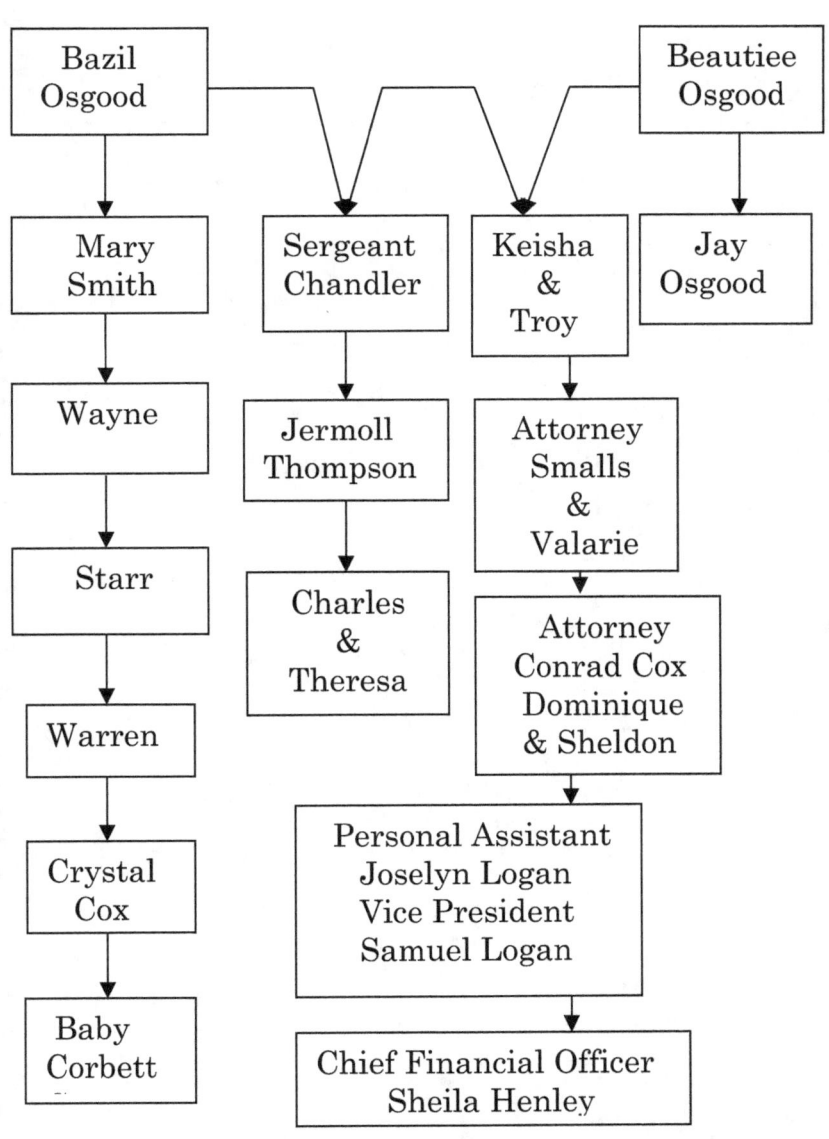